'I don't make the mistake of allowing sentiment to cloud the issue.'

'And you're saying I do?' Despite the heat, Kate shivered.

Jake gave her a long look, his expression masking whatever he was feeling. 'How long did you imagine you could go on covering for him? Pretending that everything was fine?'

'It was fine. I am a perfectly competent doctor.'

'Who doesn't belong here,' came the brutal reminder.

Her head jerked up. 'So what do you intend doing?'

His brooding gaze lingered on her flushed cheeks. 'I don't have any choice,' he said coolly. 'I'm being paid to do a job and I intend doing it, whether it's to your liking or not, Dr Tyson. I intend putting in a submission for the immediate return of both yourself and your father to England.'

Jean Evans was born in Leicester in 1939. She married shortly before her seventeenth birthday and has two married daughters and five grandchildren. She gains valuable information and background for her Medical Romances from her husband who is a senior nursing administrator.

Having lived in various parts of the country, including the beautiful Vale of Clwyd, Jean Evans now lives in Hampshire, close to the New Forest and within easy reach of the historic city of Winchester. She also writes under the pen-name of Leonie Craig.

FORTUNE ISLAND DOCTORS

BY

JEAN EVANS

MILLS & BOON LIMITED
ETON HOUSE   18-24 PARADISE ROAD
RICHMOND   SURREY   TW9 1SR

First published in Great Britain 1989
by Mills & Boon Limited

© Jean Evans 1989

Australian copyright 1989
Philippine copyright 1989
This edition 1989

ISBN 0 263 76642 X

Set in Times 11 on 11½ pt.
03 – 8911 – 50787

Typeset in Great Britain by JCL Graphics, Bristol

Made and Printed in Great Britain

CHAPTER ONE

USING her forearm to wipe away a thin film of sweat, Kate Tyson shaded her eyes to gaze up at a cloudless, blue sky, and thought of England. It was probably raining! She had never thought it possible, but she actually experienced a tiny pang of envy. It certainly had been raining on the day, some three months ago now, when she had boarded the plane which was to carry her half-way round the world, to the Pacific Ocean and a tiny cluster of atolls known as the Fortune Islands.

Completing her examination of her last patient, she listened to the gratifying sound of a healthy heartbeat and gave a smile as she let the stethoscope fall against her white coat. 'That's fine, Jacob. Much better. Your chest is quite clear. I shan't need to see you again. Oh, and . . .' she called after the retreating bronze-skinned child, 'thank your father for the fish.'

Straightening up, she eased her back and laughed as she watched him run across the sugar-white sand. 'So much for a child who, three weeks ago, was desperately ill with pneumonia.'

Maggie Smith, a tall, blonde Australian nurse, grinned as she gathered up the discarded instruments and placed them in a portable steriliser. 'Another triumph for modern medicine. They're a hardy lot, these islanders and you have to give them credit. They may not have a lot in the material sense, but they certainly have a zest for life.'

Kate gave a wry chuckle. 'Irrepressible is the word I think you're looking for, and I know what you mean. Give it five minutes and, I'll lay odds, Jacob will be diving with his mates in the lagoon.' Sitting back she wiped her face and neck, easing the coat from her clammy skin. Completing her notes she began a check of the supplies box. 'We're running low on sterile dressings again; antiseptic powder too.' She frowned. 'The way we get through it I'm beginning to think someone must eat it!'

'Well, they're welcome. I've made a note. I'll make sure it gets priority when the next order goes in.'

'I'll let you have a list of drugs and equipment as soon as I've had a chance to go through the cupboard.' She bit her lower lip. 'It's not going to be easy to keep it down to the limit. We seem to be getting through more and more.'

'Strewth, we're seeing a lot more patients. It was a struggle to get them to accept us at first, but now that they have we can hardly turn them away.'

Kate's blue eyes clouded. 'I know. I dare say I'll think of some way through the red tape. In the meantime, don't tell me we've actually seen the last patient.'

'I could probably round up a few more if you like.'

'Don't you dare! We have a hard enough time as it is, trying to convince them that this isn't the village meeting place.' Kate raked a hand through the damp curls of her long, dark hair. Even tied back as it now was, the weight of it seemed to tug at her scalp, making her head ache, yet she was loath to cut it. She flexed her shoulders, attempting to ease the tension. 'Phew, this heat.'

'Here, you'd better drink this.' Maggie poured two glasses of fruit juice from a thermos jug. 'I suppose you have been remembering to take your salt tablets?'

Kate pulled a face. 'I guess I couldn't have.'

'And you call yourself a doctor? A fine example we'd be setting if you go down with dehydration.' Reaching into a cupboard, Maggie shook two tablets out of the bottle and placed them on the table. 'You'd better take these now and I'll make sure you get another dose in a few hours' time.'

Kate didn't argue, but took the tablets and drank greedily. Even in the shade the heat was intense. The small building which housed the clinic was, like every other building on the island except the hospital, made of bamboo, while light poles, lashed together with coconut fronds, served for rafters and framework. The roof was thatched with sago palm, but at this time of day, when the sun beat down at its fiercest, it seemed to offer little relief. Even the wooden shutters at the windows flapped desultorily in a hot, sticky breeze.

It was all a very far cry from the busy casualty department at St James's, with its peeling paintwork and a perpetual smell of damp clothes and central heating. In fact, gazing out at the coconut palms and white sands skirting a blue-green lagoon, there were times, Kate couldn't help thinking, when her being here seemed nothing more than part of a dream.

'I don't think I'll ever get acclimatised.'

'Sure you will. It takes time, that's all. You can hardly compare this to your average British summer.'

'How true.' Kate gazed with envy at the tall, slim figure in shorts and cutaway T-shirt. In fact, she thought, it would be difficult to find any place on earth that could quite compare with the beauty of the tiny, reef-fringed island where time almost seemed to stand still.

She straightened up, trying to ignore the trickle of sweat that ran between her shoulder-blades. 'Was it my imagination or were there more patients than usual today?'

'It wasn't your imagination. They were queuing up outside the clinic at dawn. I must have examined a dozen babies today and there wasn't a thing wrong with any of them. In fact,' laughter twinkled in Maggie's brown eyes, 'if anything I'd say they were all disgustingly healthy. Such cute little beggars too, like bronze-skinned cherubs—most of the time, that is.'

Kate smiled wryly. 'I know what you mean about them all being disgustingly healthy. I had the same thing with the adults complaining of non-existent stomach pains. I was just about to panic, thinking we must be in for some kind of epidemic, and wondering how on earth we'd cope, with the next shipment of medical supplies not due for at least a week. Then I realised what was really happening. The only thing catching around here is curiosity. I'd forgotten you can't keep anything secret on the islands, even if you wanted to. News travels like wildfire.'

Maggie's eyebrows shot upwards. 'You mean they've heard that the big man from over the water is coming to the island?'

'Well, can you think of anything else?'

'But how? We only got the radio call a week ago, and I certainly haven't spoken about it to anyone. Strewth, I'm not looking to start a riot.'

'Let's hope it won't come to that.' Kate's voice held a note of dismay.

'Have you told your dad yet?'

'I've tried.' Kate spoke rather grimly. 'He ought to know, but his fever was up, making him slightly delirious, so he's not taken in too much of anything. Besides,' she bit her lip, 'what exactly can I tell him? We could be misjudging the situation. Just because the health organisation

choose now, of all times, to send someone out . . .'
She broke off lamely and began briskly stacking
boxes into a pile. 'Right now, my first concern is for
Dad. You know how he feels about the islands and
the people here. The idea of having to leave would
just about kill him.'

'You don't seriously think it will come to that?'

'That's the trouble, I don't know. What other
reason could there be for sending someone out?'

Maggie looked up from counting syringes into a
box. 'Surely they can't sent your dad back to
England just because he's been ill?'

They looked at each other for a long moment,
then Kate sat down heavily. 'You don't suppose
they suspect?'

'No,' Maggie said quickly. 'Why should they?'

'I've been covering for three months, without
any official blessing. I've treated Dad's patients,
signed requisitions for drugs.' Kate picked up the
remains of her fruit juice and gulped it quickly.
'I've ordered equipment.'

'So what? You're a doctor.'

'A very newly qualified doctor, who has no right
to be here, doing the job I've been doing,' Kate
said in a shaky voice.

She got to her feet, a tall, slim figure with dark
hair and a face that was gamine rather than
classically beautiful. A small, straight nose, above
a mouth that was generous but firm, and blue eyes
which were, at this moment, troubled.

'I blame myself for not realising sooner that something was wrong. If only Dad had been more of a letter-writer, but he was always too deeply immersed in his work. It was almost a standing joke between us——' Kate's voice broke. It was almost three years since her father had been offered the job as part of a huge relief organisation's medical team. Coming at a time, just two years following the death of her mother in a car accident, the offer had provided the impetus he needed to rebuild his life and, even though she was still recovering from her own sense of loss, Kate had been glad when he had told her of his decision to accept.

His initial tour of duty was for six months. No time at all, she had told herself and, anyway, she was going to be working too hard at her own medical studies to have time to miss him too much.

John Tyson's letters, rare though they had been, had given her at least a glimpse of the tiny islands, and she had become slowly but increasingly aware of his growing sense of commitment to a way of life and the islanders themselves.

What she hadn't been prepared for was his decision to stay. 'I'm needed here,' he wrote. 'There is so much to be done. These are simple, generous people, whom I can help. I have set up a small clinic, which attracts an increasing number of patients. So much so, in fact, that I am hoping, with the organisation's blessing, and money, to be able to build a small hospital.'

There had been other letters, telling her that the hospital had become a reality. Two fully trained nurses had been sent out and between them they were busy training several of the islanders to become orderlies.

Then he had had a bout of malaria. Poetic justice, he joked. After that the letters had become more infrequent and finally stopped all together.

'I knew there had to be a reason,' Kate told Maggie. 'I sensed that something was wrong. I just wasn't sure, until I wrote telling him that I'd passed my exams and qualified. He didn't answer and I knew that he would have done, if he could. My becoming a doctor was a dream we'd shared for too long for him to let it pass without at least some sort of acknowledgement. That was what made me decide to come for myself.'

'Well, I was real pleased to see you step off that boat. I'd been going on at him for ages to let me write to you, but you know what he's like—stubborn as a mule.' She flushed. 'Sorry!'

'Why be sorry?' asked Kate. 'I'd say it just about fits the bill.'

'I guess it must be a family trait.' But there was humour in Maggie's voice as she said it. 'You came in here, sized up the situation and took over without any notion of what you were getting yourself into. You didn't have any choice and you've scarcely drawn breath since.'

Kate met the Australian girl's gaze apprehensively. 'You make me sound like . . .'

'A crazy Brit?' Maggie offered. 'I don't mind admitting, when your dad went down with that last bout of malaria, I was on the point of screaming for help. We don't get many emergencies on the island, thank God, but, when we do, either we get the patient over to the big island, or he takes his chances, and I wouldn't have given much for them, to be honest, if Sue Ling and I had had to cope on our own for too long.'

'But you're both qualified nurses and very good ones.'

'Oh, sure. Unfortunately they forgot, back in Sydney, to make open-heart surgery a part of the training syllabus.' She grinned then shook her head, serious again. 'We need more trained staff, especially now that we've got the hospital. Now that Sue Ling's sick, and we've had to send her over to the big island, we're really hard-pushed. Your dad's a conscientious man. The trouble is he won't accept that he has human limitations. He thought he could be on call twenty-four hours a day, and now he's paying for it, and so will you if you don't watch out.'

'I'm fine,' Kate insisted firmly and with slightly more certainty than she actually felt. She frowned. 'There just wasn't an alternative. It seemed the easiest solution, for me to step in, just until Dad was well again. Perhaps if I'd known it would take so long . . .' She bit at her lower lip. 'He should be showing real signs of improvement by now. I don't understand why he isn't. Perhaps I'm missing something.'

'Oh, come on, you can't blame yourself. Each bout of malaria has left him progressively weaker. Then he went down with pneumonia, about a month before you arrived and it's left him pretty crook, that's all.'

'Well, he's convinced he'll be fit and working again in no time.'

Maggie threw her a sceptical look. 'Even I'd say he's being overly optimistic.'

'I figure it's better to let him go on thinking it than to disillusion him.' Kate sighed. 'None of which is going to solve my problem when this . . . this man from the organisation arrives and finds out what's been going on. I'm just going to have to face it when the time comes.' She stared blankly at the contents of her medical bag for a moment, then recalled herself hurriedly. 'I'd better take some sachets of antiseptic solution with me, and some more antibiotic tablets.' She reached up and took a bottle from the shelf and shook the contents. 'We need more supplies of penicillin too.' Tipping a quantity of the tablets into a smaller bottle, she locked the drugs cupboard then slipped out of her white coat before following the other girl out into the even hotter air that wafted in from the sea.

Within days of her arrival on the island, Kate

had quickly realised that the small collection of summer dresses she had carefully packed and brought out with her from England, while suitable for the British climate, were totally unsuited to conditions out here. Sleeves and neatly belted waistlines caused nightmarish heat rashes and she had quickly discarded them in favour of the sarong-type garment worn by the island women. At five feet seven inches tall, the fabric draped her figure, emphasizing curves far more effectively, though she was unaware of it, than any formally tailored garment could ever have done.

She gazed into the distance, shading her eyes as she watched bronze-skinned young men rowing their canoes fearlessly through a ridge of surf as it broke over a reef. At first she had watched in terror, expecting to see them thrown into the water, girding herself to deal with the major lacerations which she knew would occur from contact with the razor-sharp coral. But it didn't happen, or at least very rarely. The islanders grew up with the sea. As children they might treat it as a game, but they grew up very much aware of the dangers.

Kate's mouth compressed. 'It would kill Dad to leave all this. He's grown to love it too much. Can you imagine how he would face going back to a forced retirement in England after this?'

'I wouldn't like to put odds on his lasting a year.'

'Neither would I.' Kate sometimes wondered how she would have survived the past months without the Australian girl's cool stoicism. 'But that's what's likely to happen, unless I can do something to prevent it, and that's not going to be easy. When this man—Ramsey, or whatever his name is—arrives with his bowler hat and briefcase and finds out that I've been running things, he's not likely to be pleased.'

'What do we actually know about him?'

'Practically nothing,' Kate had to admit. 'But he must be pretty high up with the organisation. He travels all over the world in his official capacity, which presumably means meeting heads of state in countries that need relief aid, and he's a surgeon as well as a doctor.'

'Impressive.' Maggie raised an eyebrow. 'Perhaps we can lose him on one of the other islands. With a bit of luck, no one would miss him for ages—years even, if we got really lucky. Who knows, after a while he might not even want to be found.'

In spite of herself, Kate had to chuckle. 'You're incorrigible.'

'I just don't fancy seeing the doc, or you for that matter, posted back to England, just because some fella is strangled by his own red tape. Has it occurred to you that if you go the clinic and the hospital may well have to close? And if that happens these people will go back to where they were three years ago, before your dad arrived.' Maggie's mouth compressed. 'It's not on, as far as I'm concerned anyway. If matey wants to try, he'll have a fight on his hands.' She gave a snort of disgust. 'This Ramsey bloke doesn't know how lucky he is.'

'Lucky?'

'Sure. If he'd got here a hundred years ago, he could have found himself being served up as dish of the day.'

Kate grinned. 'Well, at least we've progressed a bit since then.'

'You reckon?' Maggie gave her a derisive look. 'The islanders are definitely uneasy. They don't like outsiders at the best of times, and who can blame them? They've seen what happens on the other islands once strangers move in and start trying to change things.'

'But they could hardly confuse the work the relief organisation does with that of developers.'

'Don't count on it. They're already seeing this bloke Ramsey as some sort of threat.'

Kate frowned. 'Yes, I'm afraid you're right. I'm not sure how, but somehow I'm going to have to try and put their minds at rest.'

'How are you going to do that when you don't know yourself what he has in mind?'

'I don't know, yet, but I'll think of something.' Her brow furrowed. 'I suppose I could always try appealing to his better nature.'

'You're assuming he has one,' said Maggie drily. 'You could be wrong.'

'In that case, I'll just have to think of something

else.' Kate wiped her neck and face again. 'Right now, I've got work to do.'

She waved to the tall, dark-skinned figure striding up the beach towards her. 'Nori.' She greeted the young islander with affection. At twenty-five, broad-shouldered and good-looking, he took his duties as son of the village headman very seriously. Yet at the same time there was about him a curious mingling of the old island ways and the modern, outside world. His father had been enlightened enough to send him to one of the missionary-run schools on one of the larger islands and, as a result, Nori spoke a very good, if heavily-accented, English.

'Maggie.' He greeted the other girl with a grin. 'The women in my village are hoping that you will visit and talk to them again about making babies.'

Maggie's eyebrows shot upwards. 'Oh, are they indeed!'

'I think they found it . . . most interesting.'

'I'll bet they did. As I recall, they fell about laughing, and the object of the exercise, let me tell you, was to teach them about *not* having babies. Though God knows why I bother, just because someone back home decides that family planning should be part of my official duties. These people enjoy their children. I've never seen a happier or healthier bunch anywhere, so why change things?'

Kate smiled. 'Well, if nothing else your little lectures seem to be providing a welcome source of entertainment!'

Nori's grin widened. 'The men would also like to listen.'

Maggie choked. 'I'll bet they would! I thought the typical male attitude was that this was all women's stuff.'

He spread his hands in a gesture of uncertainty. 'Now they're not so sure.'

'How's that for male chauvinism in reverse?' Kate hooted with laughter. 'Over to you, Nurse Maggie.'

Nori looked at Kate. 'You want to visit the far side of the island?'

She nodded, instantly serious. 'One of the men was fishing off the reef and injured his foot on some coral. Apparently it happened a few days ago and the wound has turned septic. I thought I'd finish the BCG vaccinations too, while I'm there. The last thing we want is to become complacent, just because the incidence of tuberculosis is falling.'

Maggie handed her a pair of surgical scissors. 'Here, you'll need these. The recorded cases of leprosy are falling, too. I've only seen one and that was treatable. God knows what it must have been like years ago when there was no treatment, except to ship the poor blighters off to some colony to fend for themselves.'

'We can thank the nuns who set up the leprosarium on the far island for that.' Kate frowned into the contents of her bag. 'Adela Kenekina had her baby two days ago. I shall need sterile powder for dressing the umbilical cord.'

'It's in there,' Maggie confirmed.

'Philemon Tafia has started her labour,' Nori said. 'She's waiting for you to deliver the child.'

Kate ceased her rummaging through the contents to look at him incredulously. 'But she's had . . . how many is it? five already. All perfectly straightforward and without any assistance from me. And now she wants me to deliver this one?'

'It's becoming quite a status symbol among the younger women to have their babies delivered by a real doctor.'

'They're all getting in on the act,' Maggie chuckled. 'They'll be demanding room service next.'

'Philemon is sure this one will be a boy.'

'Oh, is she?' Kate smiled. 'And how can she possibly know that? With five girls already, I'd say the odds are heavily against.'

Nori seemed unperturbed. 'Philemon seems to know these things. She's never been wrong yet.'

'So much for modern science.' Maggie walked with them down to the beach where a canoe was pulled up on to the fine sand. 'It seems we don't have all the answers after all.'

'Perhaps it's as well.' Nori looked at Kate as he spoke. 'It would be worse if our people had learned to expect the advantages of your medicine, only to have it taken away by someone from your side of the world who has no notion of what we want or need.'

'It may not happen,' Kate said ineffectually. 'At least it may not be as bad as . . . as you think.' Only just in time she had stopped herself from aligning her own fears to his. 'You may get a replacement doctor.'

'We have a doctor.'

Kate studied him gravely. 'We have to face the fact that my father is still very sick, Nori.'

'Will he get well if they send him back to England?'

Kate opened her mouth then closed it again, shaking her head. 'I can't say that. No one could give you an answer.'

'Then we must be sure he stays.'

Kate watched him, her expression thoughtful, as he went to drag the canoe down to the water's edge. 'Now what do you suppose he meant by that?'

'Your guess is as good as mine.' Maggie shook her head. 'How is your dad today, anyway?'

'Much the same. He woke a couple of times in the night. I think he must have tried to reach for a glass of water because I heard a crash and rushed in to find the bedside lamp on the floor and Dad, half out of bed, trying to find it. I sponged him down to try and reduce the fever and gave him some fruit juice to drink. It seems to help.' Kate sighed. 'What he seems to resent most is the feeling of weakness, the enforced idleness.'

'It takes time, he should know that.'

'He's not used to not being able to work, and what makes it worse is that he's more concerned for me than for himself. I keep trying to convince him I'm fine.'

'Look, do you want me to pop in and check on him?'

'Would you? I'll only be away for a few hours. I've tried to persuade him to let me move him to the hospital. It would be so much easier to keep a proper eye on him, make sure he takes his medication. But he's dead set against it.' Kate ran a hand over her brow. 'At least he has Selena to look after him. She's been housekeeping for him since he arrived, so she knows how to deal with him if anyone does.'

'I'll call in just the same. I'll do a ward round as well. In fact, I may do it first, so that I'm prepared when he asks the inevitable questions.'

'I should be back before sunset.' Kate climbed precariously into the canoe. 'Let's hope Philemon's first boy doesn't decide to keep us waiting, or present any complications. I'll never be able to hold my head up again if anything goes wrong with this delivery!'

'Give him a kiss from me.' Maggie waved as Nori dipped a paddle into the water, steering the canoe skilfully out into the lagoon.

Kate sat back, glad to let her thoughts drift as

they made the journey to the far side of the island. Out in the lagoon a faint breeze stirred, but it brought little or no relief from the heat, and she was glad of the straw hat she had remembered to bring with her as it shaded her from the worst of the sun's rays.

It always amazed her that the islanders could keep up the steady, paddling rhythm for hours, a relic perhaps of the old days, when they had gone out in great war canoes to carry out raids on some neighbouring island. Watching Nori, his muscles rippling beneath his bronze skin as he deftly manoeuvred the small craft through a narrow stretch of reef, it occurred to Kate that they weren't so far removed from the days of ritualistic blood-lettings. Nori's own father might even have taken part.

She couldn't help the tiny shiver of relief that ran through her that such things were now, very firmly, a part of the past!

Skirting a headland they began to move in towards the shore. Even at this depth, the water beneath the canoe was crystal-clear and Kate watched, fascinated, as a small basking shark moved lazily through the reef as if patrolling its territory, sending shoals of more brilliantly coloured smaller fish scattering. It was the larger, more deadly, white shark that struck terror into the heart whenever a tell-tale fin was sighted, though mercifully that was rare, since they seldom seemed to venture into the more shallow water which covered the reef.

A beach loomed ahead, shimmering white in a heat haze. Beneath the palms, Kate could just make out the figures, waving as the canoe drew closer. Then Nori was in the water, dragging the small craft up on to the beach and Kate climbed out, to be surrounded by giggling children who clutched at her hands and clothing. Her bag was taken from her and she was escorted up the beach to the village, where it seemed that the whole of the small community had gathered to welcome her, except that, this time, Kate sensed reserve in their greetings.

It was expected that she would put on her white coat. When she had first arrived, Kate had set up her outdoor clinic, using a small, fold-up table on which she had set out her bag, and then proceeded to wait . . . and wait . . . for the first patient to materialise. When, an hour later, not a single one had put in an appearance, she had begun to think that perhaps she wasn't welcome. It was Nori who had explained, gravely, that the white coat represented her official status. Until she put it on she was a welcome guest in the village, and no islander would approach an honoured guest with anything but hospitality. From that day, Kate had remembered her white coat. Not that it seemed to be having the desired effect today!

Trying not to notice the distinct lack of patients,

Kate gave her full attention to the wound she was cleansing. Swabs of antiseptic solution cleansed the area and she couldn't help wincing as she looked at the area of inflammation. It was a particularly nasty wound, typical of those caused by the sharp edges of coral. Its edges were jagged and raw, which would make the healing process a long one and consequently leave the man at risk from infection.

As she applied an antibiotic cream, Kate glanced up, surreptitiously, to discover that her usual, enthusiastic audience was remaining at a distance. She was puzzled. The islanders weren't usually so reticent, and had even been known to offer advice on treatment, but today they stood aloof, friendly, but seemed reluctant to approach.

Lowering her head, she completed the dressing and straightened up.

'One more.' Nori carried a small and plainly distressed little girl in his arms. She couldn't have been more than three, but already she was showing the typical beauty of all the island children, dark-eyed, dark-haired and with deep, honey-coloured skin.

'Oh dear.' Kate smiled reassuringly as her gaze went questioningly to Nori.

'A war wound, I'm afraid. Tani's big brothers were fishing. She tried to join in and one of the hooks got caught in her finger.'

'We'd better take a look.' Kate moved in without

actually touching the wound. 'I'm afraid you'll have to hold her. I'm going to have to push the hook through, it's the only way to avoid the barbs. I'll freeze it and do it as quickly and gently as possible.'

'I'm sure Tani will be very brave, like her brothers.' He smiled as he said something softly to the child in the pidgin English most of them used. She gazed tearfully at him, then snuggled close. Nori nodded. 'Go ahead.'

Kate set to work as quickly and deftly as possible. Again, it was a fairly common injury. Fishing, whether by hook or line or spear, even bow and arrow, was a common pursuit among the people, the catch varying from bonito and tuna to porpoise. Sometimes even shark and flying fish were landed, though they weren't highly favoured.

She eased the lethal-looking hook through the delicate flesh, promptly enclosed the small and surprisingly clean wound in antiseptic tissue, and grinned as she held up the offending item. 'Operation successful.'

If only she could say the same for the remainder of her visit. Clearing her instruments away, Kate stared at the troubled brown eyes all gazing solemnly in her direction. She couldn't simply pack up and walk away. Scrubbing her hands she looked uneasily at Nori. 'No more patients?'

He didn't return her gaze. 'Give them time.'

But how much time? She had treated all the

wounds, had managed to complete the programme of vaccinations and had confirmed Philemon Tafua's belief in the miracle of modern medicine by delivering a healthy, nine-pound boy. But since then, nothing.

'Something's wrong,' she said quietly. 'I can sense it. Why aren't they queuing up? Usually they'll be sitting around, telling me their news while I treat my patients.' She glanced again at the watchful, but near silent, groups.

'They want to know if it's true that the big man from across the water is coming to take Dr John away?'

Kate dried her hands, straightening up slowly. 'Nori, we don't know that it's true. I . . . tell them . . . tell them that it is true the big man is coming, but that I'm sure it's nothing for them to worry about.' She bit her lip as Nori's mocking gaze held hers.

'You want me to lie to them?'

'No!' Her blue eyes pleaded with him. 'Just . . . just explain to them that I feel sure that Dr Ramsey, when he arrives, will want what is best for them.'

'But they know what is best for them.'

'Nori,' she spread her hands in a gesture of helplessness, 'I don't know what to say to them.'

'They are worried that this man—Ramsey—will make trouble for you when he comes, when he finds out that you have taken Dr John's place. They want to know what they can do.'

'They mustn't do anything.' Alarm widened her eyes and she shook her head fiercely. 'It's my problem. I'll deal with it. Besides . . . for all we know it could be a routine inspection.' Nori raised an eyebrow and she laughed, brokenly. 'Who knows, he may even offer us a bigger hospital.'

'Is that what you believe? Am I to tell them they have no reason to fear?' He looked at her. 'I won't lie to them, Kate, not even for you.'

'I don't expect or want you to lie.' Her eyes met his in a mute appeal for understanding. 'But I don't know, any more than you do, about what may happen. I don't see what can be gained by fuelling false speculation. I care for these people, too.' She broke off, ashamed to feel tears well up in her eyes.

Nori's hand reached out to take hers and she smiled shakily, glad of its firm reassurance. 'I'll speak to them, but their concern is for you as much as for themselves.'

'I'm not important,' she said forcibly. 'I can always go back home and make a fresh start.' Not that it would be that easy, she knew. She may only have been on the island for three months, but it was long enough for her to understand how her father felt and to feel its magic for herself.

She waited, not understanding the words as he spoke to the silent group, but she sensed that he had their trust. When he finally turned to her, he gave a faint smile and she reached for her medical bag as they made to take their leave. The villagers, as always, followed them to the water's edge, but they were out into the deeper water of the lagoon before Kate distracted him.

'What did you say to them?'

Nori smiled as the paddle cut its rhythmic pattern through the water. 'I simply told them that we belong to the island and the island belongs to us.'

She waited for him to go on, but he said nothing more and Kate wondered why a tiny flicker of alarm should run through her. She shrugged the thought away, telling herself she was being ridiculous, reading more into the words than there had actually been . . .

Closing her eyes, she tilted her head back, letting the faint breeze riffle through her hair. In a lazy gesture she reached up, tugging the restraining pins from it, running her hands languorously through its thickness as it fell round her shoulders.

The sun's heat was only fractionally less as they came back within sight of the strip of pale beach where they were to land. As the water became shallow Kate rose with a grin, perching precariously on the edge of the canoe. 'Race you ashore.' Laughing, she jumped into the water and began swimming feverishly for the shore.

Nori laughed in protest, then began to dip the paddle more strongly into the water as he followed her to the edge of the sand, where he leapt out and they both collapsed into a giggling, breathless heap of arms and legs.

'I won easily.'

'I let you win,' he teased.

Kate gurgled with laughter as he pulled her to her feet and, with an easy gesture, tugged a large, white flower from one of the bushes which grew in such wild profusion all over the island.

Smiling down at her, he tucked the bloom behind her ear and drew her towards him, his hands on her hips, neither of them conscious of the way her wet sarong clung to her figure. Her relationship with Nori was uncomplicated, as were most relationships among the islanders. Trust and affection went hand in hand. Nori was the brother she had never had.

'Now you belong island too.' He brushed her lips lightly with his own.

Kate felt oddly moved by the gesture. 'Now I belong island too.' she repeated softly.

'Well, I'm glad to hear it,' a deep, masculine voice proclaimed, brusquely. 'I was beginning to think no one on the island spoke English.'

Kate would have fallen if Nori hadn't held her as she spun round, her attention riveted on the man who stood there.

For several seconds no one moved as the dark, brooding glance subjected her to a flagrantly masculine appraisal. It was as if an electric current passed through her body. It wasn't just the overwhelming sense of power and self-assurance that seemed to emanate from him as he stood there, it was something in the piercingly blue eyes which raked her slender figure and delicate features with an intensity so vibrantly sexual that it almost took her breath away.

She was immediately conscious of every line of his muscular body, from the taut shoulders beneath the open-necked shirt, to a slim waist and lean thighs beneath the jeans he was wearing. Kate found herself staring at strong, classical features and black hair which curled slightly against his neck, then suddenly she was aware, as the flush darkened her face, that the thin sarong she wore concealed nothing. On the contrary, its wetness revealed every slender curve of her body, from her tanned shoulders and breasts, to her shapely legs and hips, and his steel-dark gaze covered every inch.

Without knowing why, she sensed that this man represented some kind of threat. Instinctively her hand sought Nori's and she felt his fingers close reassuringly over hers.

The gesture didn't go unnoticed. She saw the man's eyes narrow before his gaze dismissed her and swept instead to Nori.

'I've come a long way,' he enunciated carefully,' 'to see Dr Tyson, Dr John Tyson . . . Perhaps you can tell me where I may find him, since no one else on this island seems able, or willing, to do so. My name, by the way, is Ramsey. Dr Jake Ramsey. I believe I'm expected.'

CHAPTER TWO

KATE stood, feeling the shock waves engulf her. It was *him*. Jake Ramsey.

Nothing could have prepared her for the sheer physical impact of the man. The ageing, bespectacled, dark-suited official of her imaginings was swept away in one fell swoop. This man was probably no more than thirty-five, aggressively masculine, tanned and possessed of as much charm as a panther stalking its prey! She had to resist a strong urge to run for cover as he came striding down the beach towards her. Instead, she dug her bare feet into the sand and lifted her chin rebelliously. He wasn't even due for at least another week yet. Everyone knew that the small plane which did a routine hop out from the bigger island, bringing mail and other urgent supplies, only came every ten days. He must have arrived by boat—the islanders often made the trip in canoes, risky as it was.

She felt the tension in the muscles of Nori's arm and realised that her fingernails had been digging into his flesh. The silence between them seemed to go on for ever until it was broken by Jake Ramsey as he came to a halt. A frown of exasperation drew his dark brows together.

'You do speak English? Dr Tyson? Me speak doctor?'

Me speak doctor? Kate stifled a tiny explosion of laughter as it bubbled up. She enunciated the words softly. What did he think they were? Village idiots?

Jake Ramsey's gaze sharpened. 'You know doctor? You take me see him?'

Oh, better and better. He had actually mistaken her for an islander. She was aware of Nori beside her, trying to control his own laughter, and admittedly with greater success. She had to press a hand to her mouth to suppress her own giggles as realisation dawned. In a way, she could see why he should have made the error. Her white coat was tucked away in her medical bag, which was still in the canoe, and with her dark hair and the sarong she did look much like any of the island women. Not as dark-skinned maybe, her tan had only acquired the depth of pale honey, but then, Europeans had been known to visit the islands!

In spite of any feelings of antagonism she might have felt towards Jake Ramsey, Kate's natural sense of humour was aroused. So he had thought he could sneak up on them without warning, did he? Well, two could play that particular game.

Smiling coyly, she teased a strand of hair against her cheek, beckoning him as she gestured towards the village. 'We go now. I show way.'

For a fraction of a second he seemed surprised,

then his expression narrowed. 'You speak very good English.'

'Many islanders do,' she said crisply. 'Missionaries bring schools.' Was it her imagination, or was there a sudden gleam of wariness in the eyes which locked with hers?

'When I first spoke, you didn't seem to understand.'

He was too sharp by half, Kate thought. 'We not see many strangers on island.'

'No, I don't suppose you do.' His face was expressionless as he looked down at her. 'What about your boyfriend?'

Her gaze flew to Nori. 'Boy? Oh . . .' She giggled coyly, then, summoning every word of pidgin she knew, she flung them together, spilling them out so fast that, even had they made any sense, which they didn't, she knew that Jake Ramsey wouldn't be able to understand.

Nori needed no prompting. He broke into an amiable grin and ambled off towards the canoe, and in it the medical bag he would take back to the hospital.

'He go fishing.'

Jake Ramsey's brows rose. 'How very obliging of him. Are all the young men around here so friendly?'

Kate looked sharply at him, but his expression told her nothing and she found the fact oddly disturbing. Without another word she turned and headed up the beach, her feet sinking into the sand as she made her way to the village. It was galling to find that though she hurried, bending to avoid the thick undergrowth of trees, Jake Ramsey kept pace easily, but then his legs were so much longer. Pity, she might have been able to lose him, just long enough to give her time to warn her father.

But the tall figure stayed right behind her, making her feel strangely uneasy as she became conscious of the sarong, clinging damply to her figure. He was still there when they came to the small bungalow with its neat little veranda, built by the islanders beneath the shade of the palms, to face the sea, so that Dr John could always waken to the beauty of it.

But for how much longer? Kate thought grimly, and was surprised to feel herself shiver in spite of the heat. If only she had had time to talk to her father first, to prepare him.

Half-way up the steps she paused, frowning uncertainly. 'He may be asleep.' She turned defensively to the man behind her. 'He's been ill and . . . he's still very weak.'

Jake Ramsey's blue eyes looked at her speculatively. 'I didn't know that.'

Kate wished she could have bitten her tongue out, and she felt the colour flood into her cheeks. 'Oh, he's much better now.'

I'm pleased to hear it. I've come a long way to speak to Dr Tyson.'

She stared at him, wondering whether she had imagined the very slight hint of a threat in the words before she turned away, only to be brought to an abrupt halt as a hand closed firmly over her wrist.

'Wait.' Jake Ramsey stood on the step beside her now, except that, somehow, he still managed to tower above her. At five feet seven in her bare feet, Kate felt at a distinct disadvantage, in more ways than one, as the mere contact of his hand seemed to trigger some kind of electric shock against her skin. 'I can see him alone. There's no need for you to come in.'

His voice was a soft, attractive drawl and Kate wished she could back away from the tantalising smell of expensive aftershave.

She swallowed hard. 'It's no trouble,' she said tartly. 'I was coming home anyway. I have to get changed.'

Her foot was on the step when he jerked her back to face him. His eyes narrowed. 'Are you saying you live here? With the doctor?'

She got a certain malicious pleasure out of what he was obviously thinking. 'We have a very good arrangement.' Well, it was no less than the truth!

Jake Ramsey sent her a long, searching look which sent the colour rushing more deeply into her face. 'Aren't you a bit young to be anyone's woman?'

Really, the man was too much! 'I'm twenty-five.

If it's any of your business.'

'You look about sixteen.'

It was impossible to tell from his expression, whether he was angry or simply curious. Exasperated, she tried to move away, only to feel his grip tighten.

'You may think you're a woman, but you certainly don't act like one.' His eyes glinted dangerously. 'Why do I get the feeling I'm being made a fool of here?'

Kate was about to make a biting retort when, without a word of warning, his hand came up to grasp her chin and, before she could even guess what he intended, the sensuous mouth came down on hers in a kiss which she did her best to avoid, twisting her head away, her hands pressed against his chest. For several seconds she thought she had won, but Jake Ramsey was an expert and, physically, she hadn't strength to fight him, even if she had wanted to. The warmth of his firm body, the shattering impact of the kiss, had caught her off guard.

When he finally released her she drew back, shaking as she fought to stem her threatening tears.

'I hope you're satisfied,' she choked.

'Hardly that.' His mouth twisted mockingly. 'Tell me, whoever you are,' his hand rose to touch her cheek, and she felt herself tremble, 'isn't a white flower worn in the hair supposed to denote virginity?'

For a second shock held her rigid, then she drew herself up haughtily. 'You've been reading too many books, Doctor.'

He laughed softly. 'Are you saying it doesn't?'

'Why, you——'

'Careful,' came the mocking response. 'Your accent is slipping.' He looked down at her, and his expression changed. He seemed almost shaken. 'Whatever else you may profess to be, I'll lay odds you are not John Tyson's mistress, nor any man's, for that matter.'

Kate stared at him speechlessly before saying through clenched teeth, 'I suppose you'd better come in.'

'Thank you for your very kind invitation,' he said affably, but with a distinct gleam in his eyes.

Kate gritted her teeth and ran up the steps. It seemed that she was going to have to try a lot harder if she wanted to get the better of Jake Ramsey.

Inside the bungalow was surprisingly cool. Pushing open the door, Kate stood blinking in the semi-darkness as her eyes adjusted from the brilliance outside. She frowned. 'Dad?'

Ignoring the man beside her, she moved slowly towards the figure sitting in one of the chairs. She didn't know quite what she had expected, but the sight of him, with his head resting back, his face, even in sleep, drawn with pain, seemed to make her heart contract painfully. She knelt beside him. 'Dad, what are you doing out of bed?' Her breath was released in a soft sigh of relief as the paper-thin eyelids fluttered open. 'You know you're supposed to stay in bed, and why are you sitting in the dark?'

'Kate?' He stared at her, then a smile wreathed his face. 'I must have dozed off.'

'But how long have you been sitting here?'

John Tyson shaded his eyes as she pushed open the shutters, letting in a stream of brilliant light. 'I was sick of lying in bed. I fancied a change of scene; besides, it's cooler with the shutters closed.' He winced as she folded back the last shutter, and one look at his white, drawn face was enough to tell her that he was in pain.

'Is it the headache again? Where are your tablets? Did Selena forget to give them to you?'

'Now don't fuss,' he chided gently. 'She didn't forget. I just didn't need them.'

'But you know it's important to keep up the regular dosage.' Kate tried to keep from her expression the very real concern she felt. 'I'll help you back to bed, then I'll bring you some fruit juice and your tablets.'

'Perhaps I can be of some assistance?'

The softly spoken query sent her troubled gaze winging back to where Jake Ramsey lounged nonchalantly in the doorway. Kate stared at him, and could have sworn she detected a faint tightening of the steel-hard mouth. How could she have forgotten?

'Dad, we have a visitor, from England.' Her mouth felt dry. Without being aware of it, her arm tightened protectively around the frail shoulders. 'This is Dr Ramsey.' She felt the colour rise in her cheeks as she met the sardonic gaze. Silently her eyes pleaded with him to be gentle, not for her sake, but for the sake of the frail figure she wanted so desperately to protect.

Jake Ramsey's expression was unreadable as he came forward, hand outstretched. 'It's my pleasure, sir. It's been a long time.'

Kate was aware of the sudden tensing in her father's arm as he leaned forward in his chair. 'Ramsey? *Jake* Ramsey?'

'The very same, sir.' He smiled broadly as he clasped the older man by the hand. Watching, Kate felt her hackles rise defensively.

'You two know each other?'

It was John Tyson's turn to smile. 'From quite a way back. This young man, I'll have you know, was once a star student of mine. I knew he was going to be something exceptional, even in the early days, when he first entered medical school.' His hand came up to pat Kate's. 'I take it you've met my daughter, Katherine, who insists on being called Kate.'

Kate felt her face grow hot as Jake Ramsey's eyes gleamed with a hint of malicious amusement in her direction. 'There may have been a little confusion to begin with, but I think you could safely say we've met.'

'And the pleasure was all yours,' she muttered fiercely, in a voice low enough for only him to hear.

He laughed, a deep, throaty, pleasant sound which took her by surprise and, to her horror, sent a tingle of excitement running down her spine. She drew herself up sharply. He needn't think she was fooled by all that charm.

She faced him, smiling tautly. 'Isn't it an amazing coincidence that you should be sent here, of all places, Dr Ramsey?'

'Not entirely surprising.' His voice was coolly matter-of-fact. 'In fact, it was no coincidence.'

She stared at him. Her mouth opened, then snapped to a close. This was neither the time nor the place to indulge in a battle of wills with Jake Ramsey. 'I'll get some fruit juice,' she said, in a stifled voice.

'I'd prefer coffee, if you have it. I haven't had any proper sleep for days.'

'Then surely the last thing you need is coffee?' She found herself noting the faint lines of weariness round his eyes and mouth. 'It will keep you awake.'

'I'll sleep later. There are a few things I need to do first, one of them being to find some accommodation.'

'You mean no one made any arrangements?'

A slow smile spread across the handsome features and, for some reason she still couldn't put her finger on, the vague feeling of being threatened was there again. 'Would there have been any point?'

'Probably not,' she managed, stiffly. 'We don't go in for luxuries out here. I'm afraid if you want modern hotels you'll have to try one of the larger islands.'

The arrogant smile broadened. 'That's what I figured. It's lucky I can fend for myself.' The disturbingly assessing eyes never left her. 'I can live in a tent if I have to. It certainly won't be the first time.'

'I could always see what can be arranged,' she said tartly, aware of the mocking gleam in the dark blue eyes.

'Tent? What's all this about a tent?' John Tyson demanded. 'If you're looking for somewhere to stay there's always the guest-house.'

'A guest-house.' Jake Ramsey's eyes narrowed lazily. Kate wasn't fooled in the least by the movement. She was firmly convinced there was nothing in the least lazy about Jake Ramsey.

'It isn't quite what you think, not in the accepted sense of the word.' She realised that he was laughing silently at her. 'Each village sets aside one of its houses for use by passing travellers.'

'I imagine I might qualify, don't you?' he said

easily.

'I'll see what I can do,' she said grudgingly. 'I'll get the drinks. I can take you over to the guest-house later, after I've changed my clothes.'

She almost fled from the room, slipped into her bedroom and surveyed the contents of her wardrobe with a bad-tempered sigh.

Ten minutes later she carried a tray of drinks into the room, setting them on a table just as her father said, 'But of course you must stay and have something to eat. It's no trouble, is it, Kate, my dear? Selena usually leaves something ready and there'll be more than enough. My appetite isn't what it was.'

She thought she detected just the faintest trace of amusement in Jake Ramsey's eyes as she gritted her teeth and began to pour the drinks. 'Of course you're welcome. It will be nice for Dad to have some company for a change.' He could make of that whatever he liked, she thought, stifling a tiny feeling of resentment as it welled up. She supposed she ought to be grateful for the fact that her father was actually in higher spirits than she had seen him for a long time.

Jake Ramsey accepted the silently proffered cup of coffee, studying her freshly showered figure in the pale lemon skirt and baggy top in a way which Kate found oddly disturbing. It was almost as if he guessed that she had chosen the outfit deliberately, as a marked contrast to the clinging sarong. She had also swept her hair up on top of her head, securing it with clips, except where stray wisps insisted on springing out into damp, corkscrew curls against her bare neck.

Pouring fruit juice from a large jug, she handed a glass to her father, with two tablets. John Tyson swallowed them with bad grace.

'I was saying to Jake, I imagined he'd be working in some large teaching hospital back home.'

Kate almost winced at the easy familiarity with which her father spoke. She took her own drink and sat as far as possible from the man lounging so nonchalantly in the other chair and looking for all the world as if he belonged there, with his long legs stretched out, the lean, athletic body relaxed.

'Obviously the big city didn't appeal,' she said ungraciously. 'Or perhaps there wasn't one large enough.' She smiled sweetly in Jake Ramsey's direction.

'Or you could say they were all too large.'

She found herself looking directly into the blue eyes and felt herself blush. 'Was that the case?'

He gave a fleeting smile. 'I tried it, the big city life, I mean, and I didn't much care for the feeling that I was working on some kind of conveyor belt. Patients climbed on, I did what had to be done, the patients climbed off ... It's not my idea of what medicine is all about.'

Kate found herself studying him more intently. Her hand shook as she set her glass down. 'Surely that's something of an exaggeration. Was it really as bad as that?'

'Bad enough to make me decide the time had come for me to get out. I don't fool myself that I was missed.'

Kate found herself thinking that he was wrong. She saw those long, slim fingers which had fastened over her wrist, and sensed that for all his air of casual nonchalance, Jake Ramsey was utterly competent and quite ruthless.

'It sounds rather like running away to me,' she said peevishly.

Her father gave her a surprised look. 'You wouldn't say that if you knew this young man's history,' he chided. 'He just happens to be one of the best, if not *the* best, ophthalmic surgeons in the country.'

She gulped her coffee, feeling it burn her throat. 'I didn't know that. But surely it makes the decision to . . . to simply quit and walk out, all the more irresponsible.'

'I didn't say I'd quit.' Jake Ramsey set his cup down carefully on the table. 'I just came to the conclusion that other things were more important.'

'More important than saving people's sight?' She stared at him. 'I find that hard to believe.'

He leaned forward and she saw the faint strands of grey speckling his dark hair, yet she guessed he wasn't a day over thirty-five. 'There are a lot of sick and starving people in the world. People whose lives could be made more bearable, perhaps even saved, by simple medications. The kind of simple treatments and operating techniques we take so much for granted.' His mouth was taut as he gazed fixedly at her. 'For every patient I was treating in hospital, I could treat twenty in some developing country. I decided the odds weren't very evenly stacked and it was high time someone did something about it. There were plenty of people who could do what I was doing, but not many who wanted to work without the luxury of expensive facilities which an organised health service and, sometimes, private care can provide. I'm sorry if that sounds corny. It just happens to be the way I feel.'

She gave him a hesitant look. 'So you joined a relief organisation?' She glanced at her father. His eyes were closed and she watched the even rise and fall of his breathing for several seconds before she rose to her feet. Jake followed suit.

'Not immediately. I wasn't converted on the road by some blinding flash of light.' Laughter gleamed briefly in the eyes which looked directly at her. 'You could say my conscience was stirred after a colleague I'd been working with took a year's leave of absence to go and work for one of the large voluntary organisations. Some of the stories she came back with made me sit up and realise I'd been taking the easy option.'

She knew there must be a woman . . . *women*, in

the life of a man like Jake Ramsey, though why
the idea should fill her with such a sharp sense of
disappointment was something she couldn't
comprehend. She dragged her attention swiftly
back to more relevant things. After all, what he did
with his personal life was of no interest to her
whatsoever. 'But the work you were already doing
was important.'

'I still perform surgery, when and wherever it's
needed.'

Kate wandered restlessly out on to the veranda.
With evening the air became cooler and she stood
for a moment, breathing in the heavy scent of
blossoms. She heard Jake follow her, but
deliberately she didn't turn round. 'You still
haven't explained what brings you here. Why this
particular island? Why now?'

'Why the hostility?'

This time she did spin round to face him and,
without being aware of it, she took up a defensive
stance. It was several seconds before she realised
that he was studying her appreciatively, blue eyes
searching her flushed, passionate face.

The breath caught in her throat and she
swallowed thickly. She felt dwarfed, but it
wasn't a physical thing. It was something far
less tangible, a sense of dominant masculinity
which was overpowering.

'You said your visit was no coincidence.'

His dark brows snapped together. 'I said *my*

being here was no coincidence. I picked up a file in London. I recognised the name on it, though at the time I didn't make any immediate connection between it and the John Tyson I'd known years earlier. It wasn't until I'd read through it, the background history, that I realised it must be the same man.'

'That still doesn't explain why you're here.'

'You could say that I came in answer to a request,' he replied smoothly. 'Several months ago, Dr Tyson put in a request for extra funds to set up a dispensary and an out-patients clinic.' He raised one dark eyebrow. 'Surely you knew? What else did you imagine?'

'Well, I . . . Yes, of course I knew,' she finally managed. 'I wasn't sure, that's all. I mean, I only found out about Dad's request for extra funding quite recently.' She swallowed thickly. 'There have been so many rumours.'

'I can imagine,' he said drily. To her surprise his voice became more gentle. 'How long has he been ill, Kate?'

Her eyes widened, then she turned away, only to feel his hands on her shoulders, forcing her to turn and face him. She tried to pull away, but he refused to let her.

'How long since he ran the hospital?'

'Not long,' she said sharply. 'He's had a dose of malaria, that's all. You, of all people, must know how debilitating malaria can be.'

His eyes narrowed. 'Especially if it isn't just malaria.'

'What do you mean?'

'Don't take me for a fool, Kate. Anyone can see, simply by looking at him, that your father is still a very sick man.'

'He's getting better.'

'I'd prefer to make my own judgement on that.'

She broke free of him and backed away, breathing hard. 'Dammit, are you saying that my medical judgement is unsound?'

'I'm saying it may be biased, *Dr* Tyson.'

She didn't miss the slight emphasis. So he knew! Her face twisted in some emotion he couldn't define. 'The only thing he needs is time. He's earned it,' she breathed. 'So why not let him have it?'

'Is that what you hoped to give him by coming out here? Is that how you justify it?'

'I shouldn't *need* to justify it,' she retaliated fiercely. 'A doctor was needed.'

'And you just happened to be ready and willing to step into the breach.' He smiled thinly. 'Did you seriously imagine no one would notice?'

She swallowed convulsively. 'It . . . it wasn't intended as a deliberate deception. It was only intended to be a temporary measure.' Her gaze rose to meet his. 'So what gave it away?'

'You could say thirty years.'

Kate stared at him. 'What do you mean?'

'You forgot one thing. Your father qualified before you were born.'

'Is that supposed to prove a point?' Kate glared belligerently.

'What it proves is two completely different schools of teaching—a whole generation apart.' he said in a dry tone. 'You made the mistake of ordering the very latest drugs, instead of sticking to the older, more traditional ones your father used. Drugs of which he has probably not even heard.'

She listened in dismay. How could she have been so stupid as not to have thought of that? But then, it would have taken someone with the deviousness of Jake Ramsey to spot it. She blinked hard on threatening tears. 'I suppose that's why you came. You're determined to send him home, just because he has the misfortune to be ill?' Her voice took on a note of desperation. 'If you know my father at all, you must know it will kill him if he has to leave here. He has nothing to go back to.'

Jake eyed her carefully for a few moments. 'Aren't you being a little over-dramatic?'

'I don't think so,' she said flatly. 'Just what kind of a friend are you?'

'I don't make the mistake of allowing sentiment to cloud the issue.'

'And you're saying I do?' Despite the heat, Kate shivered.

He gave her a long look, his expression masking

whatever he was feeling. 'How long did you imagine you could go on covering for him? Pretending that everything was fine?'

'It *was* fine. I am a perfectly competent doctor.'

'Who doesn't belong here,' came the brutal reminder.

Her head jerked up. 'So what do you intend doing?'

His brooding gaze lingered on her flushed cheeks. 'I don't have any choice,' he said coolly. 'I'm paid to do a job and I intend doing it, whether it's to your liking or not, Dr Tyson. I intend putting in a submission for the immediate return of both yourself and your father to England.'

CHAPTER THREE

KATE wondered, as they faced each other like wary combatants, whether the threat behind the softly spoken words was real or simply intended to terrify her. Either way it succeeded! Not that she had any intention of letting him see that.

There was something about the tall, powerfully built man, about the way he stood, about his half-cynical, half-amused expression, which seemed to invite her to challenge him. Yes, you'd enjoy that, she thought, her cheeks scarlet with indignation. Well, I'm not playing any kind of game with you, fat cat. This particular mouse has got the sense to turn and run, and hopefully live to fight another day.

Even so, her heart gave a sudden, extra beat as she looked away and bent swiftly to scoop up a batch of case files from a nearby table.

She eyed him coolly, before glancing at her watch. 'I'm afraid you'll have to excuse me. I'm already late for my round at the hospital. Perhaps we can discuss this again?' She took a deep breath and forced a smile. 'That is, of course, assuming that you want me to carry on, until my replacement arrives?'

Just for a moment she thought she detected a

gleam of amusement—or was it anger?—on the rugged features. 'You're still the doctor here, for the moment.'

But only because he had no choice; he had made that very clear. 'In that case . . .' Kate was seething as she turned to make her way towards the door.

'In that case, there is nothing further to discuss.' His slight smile seemed to mock her as he moved towards her. 'I was thinking of joining you on your round. After all, the sooner I start to get my bearings the better.'

She felt her heart thud as she faced him. Was he deliberately trying to provoke her? She returned his look steadily. 'Surely there's no rush? You've come a long way. Why not get settled in first?' She paused at the open door. 'Selena will be here shortly. She always prepares the evening meal when I'm not here. I'm sure she'll have no objection to your sharing the meal, and afterwards she can show you to your bungalow.' She managed a smile.

'How much time do you need?'

Kate frowned. 'I'm sorry?'

'To warn them, to make sure the ranks are all closed and standing firm,' he said softly.

Kate felt the heat rising in her cheeks as she threw him a disdainful look. 'I don't need to warn anyone. By now the entire island will know that the big man has arrived, and what they make of it won't be influenced by me; on that you certainly have my word.'

His dark brows rose. 'The big man?'

She swallowed hard, refusing, this time, to meet his gaze. 'It's what they call any stranger, any man, that is. It . . . it isn't intended to be an insult.'

'I'm pleased to hear it,' he said mildly. 'And what do they call you?'

She returned his look steadily. 'They call me Doctor.'

'You insist on formality?'

'Not at all,' she said drily. 'The islanders virtually insist. To have a doctor at all, out here, is quite a rarity. They see it as something of a status symbol.' She couldn't resist making the point. Her gaze fell to the one bag he was carrying, and she frowned. 'Would you like some help to collect the rest of your luggage? I can arrange it.'

'Thanks for the offer, but this is it.'

'One bag?'

'I'm used to travelling light. It means I can be ready to take off for any destination at practically a moment's notice.'

'You must travel an awful lot.' She was genuinely interested, but Jake shrugged. 'Whatever and whenever the organisation's resources are needed.' His sudden smile emphasised the lines of weariness round his eyes and mouth. 'No one can be sure where the next crisis will occur. There's always some part of the world suffering from drought or famine, or both.'

'I suppose so.'

'Besides,' he gave her a quirky little smile which, to her consternation did crazy things to her pulse-rate, 'it's surprising how much I can actually cram into this old faithful.'

It did look rather battered! 'I suppose it depends on how long you plan to stay . . . anywhere.' Kate was impenitent.

Blue eyes sparkled dangerously. 'I never make definite plans. I prefer to keep my options open, so I'm afraid, Dr Tyson, that you're just going to have to get used to having me round until I can make arrangements to get you out of here.'

'That may not be as easy as you think,' she flashed back. 'The small plane to the big island comes next week, but there's only room for one passenger then.'

'I'm well aware of that. But you're forgetting, I am here for other reasons as well. As a representative of the relief organisation, I still have to look into your father's request for extra funding.'

'Don't you mean you have to decide whether or not we justify our existence, isn't that it?' A biting edge crept into her voice. 'Well, I guess we can forget it. You've already made your opinions perfectly clear.' She glared at him. 'I can see why you enjoy your work, Dr Ramsey. Someone of your type must get a whole lot of satisfaction from wielding that sort of power, especially over a woman.'

He froze. Kate knew she had gone too far. Her comments had been completely unjustified, but nothing prepared her for the speed of his retaliation.

She gasped as his hands gripped her arms, pulling her roughly towards him. He was so arrogant, so strong, his uncompromising masculinity frightened yet, at the same time, made her shudderingly aware of his attractiveness. All trace of mockery had gone from his face now, leaving his expression taut, his mouth a grim line.

'Before you make personal judgements of that nature, perhaps you ought to know precisely what my type is, Dr Tyson.'

Kate looked into the taut features and felt a tremor of something closely akin to excitement run through her. No matter how much she might dislike Jake Ramsey, there was no denying that he possessed a kind of animal magnetism which, at any other time, she might have found hard to resist. But not now.

She tugged desperately, trying to lever him away, but the movement only brought the hard, masculine body into closer contact as he held her tighter still.

'Please . . . let me go.'

But even as she struggled to break free, his mouth hovered, swooped lower. She caught the faint smell of aftershave, was aware of the warmth of his body, then the sensual mouth closed over hers in a kiss which was the punishment he had promised and more. It was a brutal assault on her emotions. She moaned softly in protest as his hands went to her hair, twining in the thickness of it. Then he released her abruptly.

Kate drew a shaking breath, her eyes dark blue smudges in the whiteness of her face as she fought to stem threatening tears. 'Was that supposed to prove something?' she snapped.

Dark brows rose. 'Look on it as a warning. Don't play games with me, Doctor, because you won't win. Like it or not, I'm here to do a job and I intend to do it. It would be easier if we could be friends, but that's up to you. Just get one thing straight,' he said tightly. 'There are thousands of deserving causes in the world. Yours will get the same consideration as any other. No more, no less, but I promise you one thing—the fact that you're a woman won't have any bearing on my decision, one way or another. I've always made it a rule never to let personal feelings interfere with my professional judgements. I suggest you do the same, Dr Tyson.'

He was gone before she could even begin to frame a response, and Kate was left staring at the door, with the distinct impression that, somehow, she had played right into his hands.

A flicker of doubt crowded in, only to be dismissed as quickly as it rose. She might have been churlish. He *was* only doing his job. But that didn't mean she had to like it, or the man himself!

By the time she arrived at the hospital, she had

managed to bring her feelings reasonably under control. Slipping into the white coat helped. Glancing briefly in the mirror she felt pleased with the metamorphosis. The uniform helped to give her an air of poise she was far from feeling as, gathering her notes, she made her way on to the ward, her smile fixed firmly in place.

Maggie greeted her with a wry grin as she unloaded packs of sterile dressings on to a table. 'I heard the news. Nori told me when he delivered your medical bag. I take it the big man took you for one of the islanders?' She chuckled. 'I wish I'd been there to see his face when he found out you weren't. How did he take it?'

With an effort, Kate tore her mind back from the memory of a punishing kiss, feeling her colour rising as she made a business of searching in the desk drawer for something. 'I think you could say he wasn't highly amused. We can take it as read that Dr Jake Ramsey is perfectly capable of taking care of himself in every respect. He's certainly no fool.'

'Oh lor'. It sounds as if we may have underestimated him.'

'That,' Kate slammed the drawer to a close, 'has to be the understatement of the year. If he has his way, there'll be no one left to run the hospital. He's already made it quite clear that Dad and I will be the first to go. If it were humanly possible I suspect he'd conjure up a plane tonight and pilot the thing himself.' She screwed up her face. 'Come to think of it, I wouldn't even put that past him.'

'*Jeez!*'

'Precisely.' Kate thudded the report book on to the desk in added emphasis. 'And to make matters worse, he and Dad apparently know each other from way back.' She flung up a hand in a gesture of frustration. 'It was . . . galling. They greeted each other like long lost friends.'

'Well, surely that's good. He's hardly likely to send him home when he realises how badly we need him and how much he wants to stay.'

Kate took a steadying breath and reached for the report book. 'I'd like to think it was that simple, but you can take if from me that Jake Ramsey is definitely not the kind of man who allows sentiment to play any part in his plans. He makes his own rules and he's certainly not trying for any popularity awards.'

Maggie looked startled by the rare note of animosity in her friend's voice. 'You really don't like him. do you?'

Kate tried to forget the tanned features and dark, curling hair, the arrogant set of jaw. 'As a man, I wouldn't know and I'm certainly not interested,' she snapped. 'Professionally he may be brilliant, but he's as sharp as a scalpel and I suspect he won't have any qualms when it comes to getting what he wants.'

'So what do we do?' Maggie asked slowly.

'Right now we don't have any choice, and he

knows it,' Kate said flatly. 'Whatever his decision about the future of the hospital, until he makes it we have to keep things running as normal. Besides, the last thing I want is to give him any cause to find fault.'

'But if he's sending you home, who's going to run it?'

'That, I'm afraid, I can't tell you. Doubtless he'll let us know what his plans are in the fullness of time.'

Two spots of angry colour appeared in Maggie's cheeks. 'But I'd defy anyone to find anything wrong with the way you run it. This may not be one of your large teaching hospitals, but I'd defy even Dr precious Ramsey to do any better.'

Touched by the display of loyalty, Kate swallowed hard. Proving her competence as a doctor might be a matter of pride, but it wasn't the main issue and she mustn't forget that.

Gazing at the blur of notes in scrawled handwriting, she rose briskly from her seat behind the desk. 'He's quite right when he says I have no right to be here, and Dad's hardly in a position to take over. We all knew what was likely to happen.' She looked pointedly at her watch. 'Shall we get on? You must be way overdue for a break.'

Maggie took the silently offered cue. 'Sure. There aren't many changes. Just one new admission. David Tufua. He was cutting cane, and managed to slice into his leg. It's a pretty bad wound—heavy blood loss and he's still in a state of shock.'

'I'd better see him first, then.'

The wooden-built hospital, like most of the bamboo houses on the island, was one simple, long construction, divided into two separate wards by a screen.

Even now, though the sun began to set, the air was still heavy, and several of the more seriously ill patients stirred restlessly. Running a hand across her own forehead, Kate made her way between the rows of metal-framed beds, and found herself fighting a familiar sense of frustration. The wooden floor was scrubbed to pristine cleanliness; curtains, which could be drawn between each of the beds, added a brilliant splash of colour. But, by any standards, the conditions were still primitive and there were times when she had been reduced almost to tears by the lack of equipment taken so much for granted back home.

Nothing of her feelings was evident, however, as she exchanged a smiling greeting with the occupant of each bed in turn, until she came to where David Tafua lay unmoving on his own bed.

Kate moved aside the thin gauze of the mosquito net and gazed down at him. He couldn't have been much more than twenty years old. She remembered him now. He was a popular young man, tall, good-looking as most of the islanders were. She had seen him often, on the beach or in the village, usually surrounded by girls.

Kate watched the rise and fall of his shallow breathing as her eyes made a quick, but thorough, assessment. She reached for his wrist and felt the thready pulse. A fan whirred steadily beside the bed.

'He's burning up with fever.' She took the notes Maggie proffered, glancing through them before handing them back, to study the injured leg. Accustomed as she was to dealing with casualty cases, the extent of the wound made her bite back an involuntary exclamation of horror.

'The knife went into the bone.' Maggie murmured softly.

Kate nodded, checking the drip. 'You've started him on antibiotics?'

'Straight away. Booster dose to begin with.'

Frowning, Kate reached for the notes again. 'We may have to change them. It's a bit too soon to tell properly yet, but I would have expected his temperature to have fallen. On the other hand, he's pretty badly shocked. Let's up the dose of pain-killers. He's very restless and the last thing we want is to have him moving about too much.' She looked at her watch. 'In fact, we'll give him another dose now.' She filled a hypodermic syringe, watching carefully for any signs of reaction as she gave the injection. 'Keep an eye on him. It's possible some infection could set in.'

She drew back, dragging her hand across her brow. 'If only we had more facilities. He'd be better off in a proper hospital, they could do so much more for him.' Her throat felt dry. 'He could even lose that leg.'

'Don't think about it.' Maggie followed her as she moved away from the bed. 'It may not happen.'

'You're right.' Kate released a long breath, and nodded. 'It's crazy to start jumping fences, but there are times when I feel so helpless.' For those few seconds she had been made starkly aware of her own vulnerability, found herself longing for someone to fall back on, to draw strength from. If only her father were well enough to take over again. But it wasn't her father's image which her mind conjured up as she scrubbed her hands with far greater ferocity than was warranted, in an attempt to shut out the all too disturbing memory of startlingly blue eyes, and a mouth twisted in faintly sardonic amusement before it brushed against hers.

'Are you OK?'

Kate drew herself up sharply, realising with a sense of annoyance that Jake Ramsey had managed to intrude into her thoughts yet again without invitation. 'What? Oh yes, I'm fine. Shall we see the next patient? Then perhaps you can go off-duty. You look as if you could do with a break.'

Maggie hooted with laughter. 'And when did *you* last take a look in the mirror, sleeping beauty?'

'As bad as that?' Kate gave a husky laugh. 'Maybe Sue Ling will soon be better—the last thing we needed right now was to have our only other qualified nurse go down with measles, of all things!' She straightened up, easing her white coat from a damp patch on her back.

Maggie measured out doses of medication before wheeling the trolley towards the next bed. 'Let's just be grateful that there don't seem to be any new cases now, and at least six of the kiddies can be released in the next couple of days. That should ease things a lot.'

Kate smiled at the next patient, an elderly man brought in a week earlier, suffering from chronic bronchitis. With Maggie's help he sat up, submitting passively as Kate made a brief but thorough examination and listened to the whistling sounds of congestion in his lungs.

Glancing at Maggie, she gave a barely perceptible shake of her head before removing the stethoscope from her ears. The old man lay back, closing his eyes, and Kate gently rearranged the sheet before drawing the curtain round the bed again.

'Why won't he let me help him?' she asked tautly. 'If he would only take the antibiotics——But I can't seem to get through to him.'

'It's not your fault.' Maggie countered. 'Some of the older people still mistrust our modern medicines.' Moving to the next bed, she cut open a sachet of antiseptic solution, emptying it into a basin as she prepared to cleanse an infected leg wound. 'They'd rather go to the village medicine man. They really believe he has magical powers.'

'Well, the medicine man certainly hasn't done much for Ariki Rua's bronchitis.'

They moved through to the women's ward. An ancient fridge whirred noisily in the corner. From it Maggie took a large jug of water, using it to refill jugs at each bedside.

Kate made her examinations, taking long enough to chat to each patient in turn. In general the women were a noisy, cheerful group who had naturally assumed responsibility for the children who needed to be admitted. They sat on their beds, chatting irrepressibly, for all the world as if it were a village meeting.

'Well, at least we have no major problems here.' Kate straightened up from her examination of a small baby, gave it a cuddle before handing it back to its mother, then began kneading the muscles at the back of her neck in an attempt to relieve some of the tension. 'Have we seen everyone?'

'That's the last.'

'In that case, why don't you go off-duty now?'

'How about you?'

'I'll be fine. Besides, there's a mountain of paperwork I need to catch up on. I've been putting it off, but I have to face it some time.'

'Your Dad wasn't exactly keen on that side of things,' Maggie confessed ruefully, as she followed Kate to the office. 'Anything even remotely official-looking usually got pushed into a drawer.'

'So I discovered, once I started trying to put

things into some sort of order. He didn't even have any kind of filing system.'

'Oh, he had a very good one. He filed everything under tomorrow. He couldn't see any need for urgency. He wasn't here to do paperwork, he was here to cure people, he always said, and there was always plenty for him to do.'

Kat's tone was subdued as she entered the small office. 'Unfortunately, I don't think Dr Ramsey is likely to accept that as any excuse.' She sighed. 'I'll just have to make a start so that at least it looks as if some attempt has been made to keep things in order. Who's the auxiliary tonight?'

Maggie reached for a list. 'Timothy.'

'Oh, well, in that case we can relax. He's a good worker. In fact, I wish he could do his proper training. He'd make a first-rate nurse.'

'You'd have to persuade his family first, and that wouldn't be easy. They see too many of the younger generation leaving the islands.'

'I know, and I don't really blame them. But I may try anyway.' Reaching the office, Kate lit the lamp and turned the fan towards her desk. Darkness came swiftly in the tropics, bringing with it the fluttering of wings belonging to a myriad assortment of insects and colourful moths.

Maggie eventually took her leave, and Kate sat at the desk, drawing a large box-file towards her. She gazed disconsolately at the bundles of unanswered correspondence and was surprised to feel the unexpected sting of tears in her eyes.

What was the point of it all anyway? She rested her head in her hand. If Jake Ramsey had his way, there would be nothing left of all the things her father had worked so hard for. What would happen to the islanders if the tiny hospital had to close? In four years they had learned that a simple injection could save the lives of their children, and that malaria needn't kill. Tuberculosis, once rampant in the islands, was now a rarity. Yet suddenly it all seemed to count for nothing.

Slowly Kate straightened up. Exhaustion seemed to descend like a huge wave. She found herself fighting the heaviness which was threatening to close her eyes. There was still the report to write up, forms to be filled in, requisitioning new medical supplies. But would anyone be here to use them? Her fingers tightened on the pen and she pressed a hand to her aching brow. The wards were quiet, almost too quiet. It gave her too much time to think, and her thoughts turned infuriatingly to Jake Ramsey, which was ridiculous, she told herself, making a determined effort to quell an over whelming desire to weep.

She brushed her hand weakly against her forehead. Her face felt dewed with sweat. She had to swallow several times before the dryness in her mouth passed. She was tired, more than tired—exhausted by the heat and the worry of her father's illness, and now the added tension of Jake

Ramsey's presence. She leaned back, easing the aching muscles in her back, then gave a startled gasp as a tall figure stepped out of the shadows.

'I saw the light on. I didn't mean to startle you.'

Kate was on her feet, conscious of the colour rising in her cheeks. How long had he been standing there? she wondered. He moved to lean nonchalantly against the locker while his gaze studied her face intently; his presence seemed to fill the small room.

'Do you usually work so late?'

'Only when it's necessary.' She tried to keep her features impassive. 'I was catching up on some paperwork. I'm afraid it's been somewhat neglected of late and it tends to build up.'

His eyes narrowed. 'Another few seconds and you'd have been asleep.'

'Nonsense.' His nearness was unnerving and her feeling of panic increased as he moved closer. In a swift movement she gathered up the scattered papers from her desk, dropping them into a drawer. 'The light was too bright, that's all. It was hurting my eyes. Besides,' her chin rose, 'I've always believed in order. It makes things so much easier for other people when they have to take over, and I'd say that was very appropriate right now, wouldn't you, Doctor?'

For a long moment she held her breath as Jake's eyes glinted dangerously. 'Just what are you trying to prove?'

'I . . . I don't know what you mean.'

'Oh, I think you do.' He had moved closer, a derisive smile touching his lips. 'I'm impressed by such apparent dedication, but if it's supposed to reinforce my own part as villan of the piece, I'm warning you, Kate, it won't work. It certainly won't influence the facts that go into my report.'

She had to suppress an overwhelming desire to tell him that she didn't give a damn what went into his report. Right now her most urgent priority was to stay upright on legs which suddenly seemed to be having difficulty supporting her. She wished he would go away before she fainted into a heap at his feet and made a complete fool of herself!

'I hate to disappoint you, but as it happens, I really do have work to do,' Kate said tersely. 'As for trying to impress you, why would I waste my time, when you've already quite clearly made up your mind that Dad and I are both thoroughly dispensable?'

There was a sarcastic edge to her voice, which she was pleased to see found its mark as he frowned. Strangely enough, she no longer cared if he was angry. It was probably one of the side-effects, the more dangerous side-effects, of being so tired that a kind of light-headedness was taking over, making her almost reckless. 'Perhaps you'd also like to include in your report that our only other qualified nurse is also sick. You may be able to get a replacement for her or, better still, it may give you even more ammunition to close us down, because that's what you'd really like, isn't it? It should help to save your precious funds.'

There was a long pause, during which he looked at her before she had to turn away, pretending to tidy the papers on her desk, rather than let him see the tears of angry frustration which welled suddenly in her eyes.

She heard him swear softly, then his hands came to rest on her shoulders and he was pulling her roughly to face him.

'Stop it, Kate. You're hysterical.'

She blinked hard, hating him intensely, yet wishing she could cry on his shoulder. Perhaps she was hysterical. Her head went back, half expecting him to apply the appropriate treatment! But he stood, looking at her, seeing the taut lines of strain, and his eyes narrowed.

'You little fool. Don't you know better than to overtire yourself in this heat?'

Of course she did. What did he take her for? A silly little student nurse? She began shivering violently, breathing in the scent of him, warm, masculine, firing all her senses. Love him or hate him, Jake Ramsey was the most dangerous man she had ever met and—the thought hit her like a cold wave—whatever else she felt for this man, it certainly wasn't hate!

She tried to pull away. 'I'm perfectly all right.'

'Like hell you are!' His searching gaze took in the deathly whiteness of her face, and his mouth took on an ominously angry look as he removed the papers firmly from her nerveless fingers. 'Just what the hell makes you think you'd be capable of taking over permanently? You don't have the experience——'

'I can learn,' she interrupted him, though the plea was scarcely more than a whisper.

'What use is a doctor who's dead on her feet? I don't suppose you've even remembered to take your salt tablets?'

Her mouth opened on a protest, only to close again as the room began to spin. 'I . . .'

'When did you last get a good night's sleep?' he asked grimly. 'I mean a proper night's sleep.' He wasn't even giving her a chance to answer. 'Here, take these.' Two tablets were thrust into her hand followed by a glass of juice. His hand was at the back of her head, the other practically forcing the liquid down her throat. He was a bully—There was no other word for it, but she felt too tired to argue.

'I've already taken my salt tablets,' she said feebly.

'I didn't say that's what they were. They'll help you to sleep.'

Indignation darkened her cheeks, but he ignored it, removing the glass briskly from her hand. 'As from tomorrow, your father will be moved to the hospital.'

'But you can't——'

'I can and will.' To her surprise, his voice suddenly became more gentle. 'I've already discussed it with him, Kate, and he's agreed.'

'I . . . He has?' She eyed him warily.

'No pressure was applied.' The note of sarcasm told her that he had read her thoughts. 'Apart from the fact that it means he can be properly looked after, and given his medications when they are due, it also means that you'll be able to get sufficient rest in order to be able to do your job.'

Oh, yes, of course, she might have guessed that his motives would be purely professional. She stiffened. 'I wasn't aware that I hadn't been doing my job, but if you have any specific complaint . . .'

He stared at her calmly. 'If I had any complaints, you can be sure you'd be the first to know. And now, instead of spitting fury like a kitten with its fur ruffled, I suggest you go to bed, before those tablets start to work, and get some sleep. I've arranged for someone to sit with your father tonight.'

Her lips compressed. He really was the most infuriating man she had ever met. 'You seem to have thought of most things, but that doesn't mean——'

'*I* will take over here, at least until the patients are settled for the night and an orderly can take charge. Should an emergency arise later I'm within easy reach.'

Kate's eyes glazed over. She felt much too weary to fight a battle they both knew she wouldn't win. She was at the door when his voice halted her.

'Sleep tight, Dr Tyson. I'd like to make an early

start in the morning.'

He was half sitting on the desk. He had extraordinarly long legs, she thought. Then he moved and her glance rose guiltily to become a frown.

'Early start?'

'Yes, did I forget to mention it?' He was sitting behind the desk now, looking surprisingly at home. 'I need to do a tour of the island. I can hardly sent back a detailed report of what's needed until I've seen for myself.'

She took a deep breath. 'What sort of thing?'

'I take it you hold clinics in each of the villages?' His gaze rose. 'Or do the islanders come to you?'

'I go to them. I try to visit each village in turn at least once a week.'

'In that case, I'll join you. Unless you have any objections, of course?'

Kate could think of plenty, but none she could voice. Her chin rose. 'None at all.'

He nodded and turned away, his attention already elsewhere. 'Goodnight then, Kate, and sweet dreams.'

Or did she only imagine that she had heard him say that?

CHAPTER FOUR

THE lagoon lay calm and still next morning when Kate made her way to the hospital. Only the tell-tale wake of white surf gave evidence of the reef lying beneath. The beauty of it never failed to stir her, but today it was as if uncertainty gave a new and more poignant edge to her feelings.

It was the coolest part of the day. A warm breeze ruffled the palms surrounding the clearing where the hospital block stood. A smell of cooking wafted from the small kitchen where patients' meals were prepared, though some preferred to have food brought in by relatives, and it wasn't unusual to see a group gathered around the beds, as if it were a communal picnic.

Kate did nothing to discourage the practice. It might not do in a large teaching hospital, but this was an altogether different world, and besides, it eased the strain on their own meagre resources.

It was only as she ran up the steps, bidding a cheerful good morning to one of the boys who came in to mop the floors, that she realised, with a totally irrational feeling of resentment, that Jake Ramsey had been right. She did feel better for a good night's sleep, the first in a long time, and her father had seemed brighter, too. He had certainly shown no signs of regretting his decision to be admitted to the hospital, for which she supposed she did owe Jake a certain debt of gratitude.

Walking into the office, she found Nori waiting for her. He had discarded his jeans in favour of a pair of brightly coloured shorts. He took in her own white coat, and raised an eyebrow quizzically. 'You're not ready. Am I too early?'

Kate looked at him in consternation. 'Oh, Nori.' The arrival of Jake Ramsey had somehow swept everything from her mind. She had completely forgotten that they had made a date to go fishing from the reef. 'I'm sorry, I should have let you know, but . . . I'm afraid I can't make it after all. I have to work.'

He smiled, but she sensed his disappointment. 'This is the best time of day to see the colours of the reef.'

'I know, and I've looked forward to it for ages.' Her voice was heavy with regret. 'I wish I could leave everything and come with you, but I have no choice. Dr Ramsey wants to visit one of the villages, to see how the clinics are run.'

'But it was to have been your first day off.'

'I know,' she sighed. 'Unfortunately I can't do anything about it. It is still my job and, in a way, I want him to see just what kind of work we do here, and how much of it is due to my father.'

She was unaware of the look of anxiety which briefly clouded her eyes. Nori moved forward, placing his hands on her shoulders as he studied her face. 'It doesn't matter. We can arrange another time, and look for turtles on the beach instead.' His hands tightened briefly on her arms. 'This man, Ramsey, does he trouble you? If so——'

'No!' Kate blushed furiously. Turning away, the began to check boxes of supplies before packing them into the large, insulated bag which she always carried with her when doing clinic rounds. At least it gave her an excuse to look away. Not that she had actually lied, she told herself. Jake Ramsey wasn't bothering her, at least, not in the way Nori meant.

'I guess I'm just a bit edgy, that's all.' Forcing a smile, she began rifling through the cupboard for packs of sterilised dressings, piling them on to the desk.

'Your father, he is worse?'

'No, oh, no. But he isn't any better either. Dr Ramsey has managed to persuade him to come into hospital so that we can keep a better eye on him.' She frowned down at the boxes on the desk. 'I don't know why, but he certainly isn't making the progress he should be making. It's . . . so confusing. Perhaps I'm not being objective enough . . .'

Nori was watching her closely. 'What will happen to you and the doctor?'

'I don't know Dr Ramsey's plans.' She was deliberately brisk, but Nori was looking at her in a way that made her feel guilty. 'He's here to do a report, but . . . I rather imagine we'll be sent home as soon as it can be arranged.'

'And the hospital? What will become of it if you go?'

She shook her head, her hands tightening over the box of drugs she was holding. 'I don't know.' She tried to force a smile. 'But I don't think you should worry about it. I'm sure I won't have any trouble convincing Dr Ramsey that it provides a valuable service. I'm sure a replacement doctor will be found.'

'Is that what you want? What your father wants?' he asked gently.

'We aren't important. Any doctor can run the hospital. What matters is that we persuade the organisation, through Dr Ramsey, that it is vital to keep it open.' She began counting vaccines, frowned and re-counted, knowing that she wasn't even taking in what she was doing. In the end she abandoned the attempt. 'Whatever happens you must help me to persuade the islanders that it will be for the best, for everyone.'

'They know what is best. They want the hospital. If they can't have Dr John, they want you.'

Kate stared at him, and felt her eyes blur with unshed tears. 'Unfortunately, it's not my decision to make, and Dr Ramsey is only doing his job. You do understand that?' She resumed her packing with shaking hands.

'I'll tell the villagers what you say, but they must judge for themselves.' His hands briefly rested on her shoulder, and instinctively Kate let herself relax against him, welcoming the feeling of protectiveness. It only she could close her eyes, and wake up to find that the past few days had all been a dream, that things were just as they had been before Jake Ramsey had walked into their lives.

'I hate to intrude.' The deep voice came from behind her and Kate broke away, spinning round to find herself staring into an all too familiar face. Jake Ramsey stood in the doorway. It wasn't only the aggressive stance which took her breath away, it was the raised brows, the derisive smile which played around his lips, as he said tersely, 'I take it you're ready. I'd like to get started as soon as possible.'

Kate silently ground her teeth. And to think that only seconds before, she had actually been trying to defend the man!

There was a distinct chilliness in her voice as she reached for her bag. 'You weren't intruding, Doctor, and yes, I'm quite ready. I had to write up the day's medications, and leave a message explaining my absence. But that's all dealt with.' She handed Nori a note, unaware that a smile briefly took the tension from her features. 'Will you see that Maggie gets this, and I won't forget that date.'

'When you've managed to separate your professional life from your busy social activities, Doctor, I'll be waiting outside.' With a thunderous look in her direction, Jake Ramsey turned and strode towards the door. 'I leave in two minutes, with or without you.'

Kate's first impulse, as she stared at the retreating figure, was to tell herself that he could go to hell and good riddance. After all, it wasn't as if she had done anything, that she was aware of, to provoke his sudden display of irritation. But then, she realised, that was probably just what he was waiting for, it would look very good in his report.

Her chin rose stubbornly. Well, she wasn't about to give him that satisfaction. He might have the power to send her home, but he wasn't going to find it so easy to fault her competence as a doctor.

He was standing beside the ancient Land Rover when she went out minutes later, carrying her medical bag. For a few seconds his gaze seemed to linger on the trousers she had elected to wear. They might be hot and not very fashionable, but at least they offered some protection to her legs against the insects which were so prevalent and voracious in some of the more overgrown areas of the island. She had chosen the pale, mint-coloured shirt for the same reason; its turn-back cap sleeves left her arms exposed, but her neck and shoulders remained protected. Her hair she had simply twisted into a heavy coil, securing it on top of her head with clips, and she became suddenly aware, beneath that cool gaze, of the escaping tendrils.

Rebelliously she pulled an ancient straw hat down on her head.

'Is this the best transport you've got?' Jake took her bag, placing it on the seat before taking her hand to help her climb in, slinging his own gear into the back before getting in beside her.

'It's the *only* transport.' Kate felt a certain malicious satisfaction as she said it.

A flicker of disbelief crossed his tanned features as he started the vehicle. Kate supposed it *was* rather ancient. Come to think of it, she had never known quite how or when it had got to the island in the first place. Presumably some previous visitor to the island, a missionary, or teacher maybe, had had it shipped out and had simply left it behind. A supply of petrol arrived in much the same way, whenever they thought to order it and someone could get it out to them. No one looked a gift horse in the mouth.

A tiny grin played around her mouth as she cast a look in his direction. 'I suppose you're accustomed to driving something rather more exotic. Would you like me to drive?'

'I'll manage.' He started the engine which, amazingly, obliged first time. Perhaps it recognised a masterful touch.

Kate hung on as they set off. 'It may be old, but it serves its purpose,' she said. 'The alternative is to walk, which I wouldn't altogether recommend. The island may be small, but some of the tracks are not so good and the vegetation is pretty dense in places. To get to the far side of the island we go by canoe.'

He shot a quick glance at her. 'Isn't there a danger from hidden reefs, not to mention sharks?'

'Not if you know what you're doing, and the islanders do. They know exactly where the dangers are, and take care to avoid them.' Sensible people, she thought, settling herself deliberately as far from the lean, tough body beside her as the confines of the small vehicle would allow. She turned, surreptitiously, to study his profile, and was devastated to meet his blue eyes. There was an expression in them that was hard to read, and she wasn't at all sure she wanted to try.

He turned away to concentrate on keeping the vehicle steady on the track and her gaze returned to his profile. The dark hair curled very slightly against the collar of the khaki shirt he was wearing. Behind his rugged face and slightly sensual mouth was a streak of arrogance, she thought. Jake Ramsey could be quite ruthless, of that she had no doubt.

'I had quite a long talk with your father last night, after you'd gone over to the hospital.'

Kate looked up at him. 'You must have done, to be able to persuade him that he should be admitted. I'm still surprised, though. He hasn't exactly been communicative of late. In fact,' she hesitated, 'I've almost had the impression that he's been deliberately shunning company, even mine.'

Jake didn't answer immediately. He needed all his concentration to keep the Land Rover on the narrow track, but she saw him frown briefly. 'It could be that you're imagining it. Or he may simply be tired.'

'I suppose you could be right.' But it didn't tally somehow with her own observations, she thought uneasily. As a doctor she had been trained to watch for the slightest reaction or variation in a patient's behaviour.

'He seemed lucid enough, even talkative, last night.'

'Perhaps it was the company,' she said bitingly.

He smiled faintly at that. 'We managed to do a lot of catching up on old times. There's certainly no memory impairment, no confusion.'

Kate felt absurdly pleased. He hadn't dismissed her fears out of hand. He even seemed concerned. 'So what did you think? You must have formed some impression of his general condition?'

'His general condition, yes. Malaria is one of those debilitating conditions that can keep recurring, yet I'd say he is improving.'

Relief sprang into her eyes. 'You really think he's getting better?'

'I didn't say that.'

'But . . .'

'I said he seems to be getting over the malaria. He's a long way from being well.'

'So what do you think is wrong?' Kate enquired uneasily.

'I'd have to carry out a proper examination before I could even begin to answer that.' He glanced up. 'What about you?'

'That's the trouble, I'm at a loss,' she answered frankly. 'I've done all the routine tests, or at least those I'm able to do with the limited facilities we have available.' She bit her lip, aware of the implication that could be read into her words. His face remained impassive enough, however. 'His bronchial congestion seems to be responding to antibiotics . . .'

'But you still feel there's something wrong?'

'Well, if there is, I certainly can't pinpoint it,' she admitted flatly. 'Maybe I'm worrying over nothing, being over-protective.'

'It's possible, but it won't do any harm to do a little discreet investigating,' he suggested mildly. 'If nothing else, it may help to put your mind at rest.'

She would have to watch out, Kate told herself, or she might be in danger of thinking that Jake Ramsey was actually quite nice after all.

She sat back, noting the damp patches darkening his shirt, and became uncomfortably aware of a trickle of sweat running down her own back. What a sight she must look. She had given up wearing make-up. In this heat there was no point.

Leaning an elbow against the open window,

Kate wiped her face and neck, easing her shirt from her clammy skin. Without warning the Land Rover lurched as a wheel hit a rut, sending her sprawling against him.

Kate gasped as her body made solid contact with his chest, knocking the air from her lungs. She heard him grunt as he slammed on the brakes, then his arm came round her shoulders, steadying her. Her whole body quivered with reaction, and his arms tightened.

'Are you all right?'

For a few seconds, as she lay crushed against him, a sensation of exquisite pleasure shafted through her, taking her completely by surprise. She tried gulping in air, willing her heart to stop its wild pumping, and nodded, wondering why there was just the slightest suspicion of a grin on his face.

'Here.' Before she knew what was happening, Jake was tugging at the collar of her shirt, fumbling with the buttons. With a tiny cry of protest she made a feeble attempt to stop him.

'What are you doing?' How dare you?' She pushed him firmly away.

'As you wish,' he murmured, a gleam in his deep-set eyes as he slowly backed away. 'But don't say I didn't try.'

Her glare of fury became one of wariness as his gaze seemed to slide down the hollow of her throat, then, with a cry of horror, she looked down and saw her bra-less figure exposed. The buttons must have come undone as she fell.

'You have a very nasty, suspicious mind, Dr Tyson,' he murmured smoothly, as he began calmly refastening the buttons. His hands brushed gently against her warm skin, and she despised herself for the way her heart hammered.

She pushed him away, scrambling with undignified haste, back to her own side of the seat. His nearness was having a disturbingly physical effect on her nerves. 'I can do it.'

His twisted smile told her that he was well aware of the panic his action was creating. 'I am a doctor, you know. I've seen the human body before.' Maybe, she thought, but not mine! 'Yours is beautiful, why be shy about it?'

Their eyes met. As his gaze held hers, she became uncomfortably aware of the dangerous qualities of this man.

'I'm not shy,' she said sharply. 'You took me by surprise, that's all.' Her buttons refastened, she felt safer, but not as safe as she would have liked.

Kate fumbled clumsily for the door handle, trying to wrench it open, but for some reason it seemed to remain stubbornly stuck. Jake's arm came round her, the contact sending a kind of electric shock running through her; then his fingers closed over hers. 'No need to panic. Let me do it.' He flicked the lever and the door fell open. He gave her a quick glance, a half-smile tugging at his lips. 'I don't bite, you know!'

Kate shot out, planting her feet firmly on the ground before she gave him a look. 'No, but I might! Now shall we get on, Dr Ramsey? We have to walk from here, anyway.' Without giving him a chance to reply, she reached for her bag, hitching it over her shoulder.

A funny sound, which might have been a cough or could have been a chuckle, came from him, but Kate didn't stop to find out. From the corner of her eye she was aware of him following. She couldn't see his face as he reached for the rest of the gear. She had the distinct feeling, however, that had she been able to, she would have found him laughing silently at her expense!

Without a word Kate set off along the track which led to the village, holding the bag securely on her shoulder as she brushed aside over hanging branches and thick undergrowth. At one point she thought that she heard a sharp exclamation of pain. She pressed doggedly on. She wasn't wasting any sympathy on Jake Ramsey. He didn't need it, she assured herself grimly. He hadn't been invited but, since he was here anyway, he could jolly well take care of himself.

To Kate's disgust, he was actually ahead of her as they came closer to where the village was situated, and she was slightly breathless as she found herself struggling to keep up. If anything, the sun's heat was stronger as the breeze which brought some relief dropped, leaving the air strangely heavy and still.

Her foot struck a dead branch, causing her to stumble. For a moment she paused to lean against a tree, only to straighten up quickly as he came to a halt some distance ahead.

He reached out for a bag she was clutching. 'I'll take that.'

'I can manage,' she murmured, rubbing one painful shin against her other leg. 'It's not heavy, just awkward.'

'Either way,' he said calmly. 'I was thinking of the vaccines. If they get broken it could take weeks to replace them.'

Unwillingly, Kate let him take the bag. Avoiding his gaze was easy, as he was taller and the brim of her battered, straw hat shaded her eyes, but she didn't miss the red weal across his cheek where a branch must have caught him full force.

'You should put something on that,' she told him, her concern genuine. 'Even minor cuts and grazes can turn septic out here if they're not treated.'

'I think I'll live,' he said mildly. 'But if you're offering——'

'I wasn't,' she said. 'I'll find you some antibiotic cream and a mirror later.'

She heard the soft rumble of laughter in his throat as he turned away, and she walked along the track behind him. Beneath the thin shirt his powerful shoulder muscles moved in taut definition. The khaki slacks hugged lean hips and thighs, emphasising his maleness. How could a man like that not be aware of his own sensuality? Or perhaps he was sufficiently experienced to know exactly what effect it could produce, an inner voice warned.

He came to a halt again as they reached the edge of the clearing. 'Just one thing, before we go in,' he said evenly. 'Let's drop the doctor bit, shall we? You'd better get used to calling me Jake.' He smiled directly at her with eyes that had all the mesmeric qualities of a snake's. 'Give it a try. You might find it surprisingly easy.'

All too easy, came the disturbing thought. Kate shook her head obstinately, resenting even the implied intimacy that the use of his name would bring. 'I'd rather not. I . . . I can't.'

'Yes, you can,' he said evenly. 'I don't want these people to see me as public enemy number one. I'm here to do a job, that's all.'

'Oh, I see. You mean we should love you for your personal charm?'

'I hadn't realised it would be quite so difficult,' Jake said gravely.

Kate shot him a quick look. Was he being serious? His mouth twisted mockingly. 'You don't know yet how persuasive I can be,' he drawled softly. 'When I want something badly enough, I usually get it.'

Kate resolutely ignored the gleam in his eye.

Why did she get the impression that he had just delivered some kind of personal challenge? It wasn't even as if she was the one he had to win over.

'Just don't hold your breath,' she muttered irritably, stumbling as her feet sank into the fine sand.

Jake's hand steadied her. She tried to pull away, but his grip firmed, and she was shaken by the feeling of warmth and strength that seemed to run through her. A little confused, she lifted her face involuntarily to his, a strange new kind of awareness bringing the faint colour to her cheeks.

'I don't want to be your enemy, Kate,' he said softly.

She didn't want to be his enemy either. Suddenly she wasn't quite sure what she wanted from Jake Ramsey.

CHAPTER FIVE

'ARE you sure you didn't arrange this?'

Kate didn't look up from what she was doing. 'Sorry?'

'Does your clinic usually attract this kind of attention? Right now it seems to be the event of the week for entertainment value.' There was a hint of gruffness in Jake's voice, and his evident annoyance puzzled her, though it appeared to be directed at something other than herself.

She finished the dressing she was working on, before releasing her patient and following his gaze. Doing a rapid mental count, her own feeling of consternation rose. She guessed that most of the village residents had turned up and were either sitting, squatting or standing in a roughly formed half-circle, giggling behind their hands as they craned their necks to see what was going on.

'What are they saying?' Jake enquired.

Without raising her head she tuned in to the pidgin, and felt her cheeks grow warm. 'It's just village gossip. Nothing you'd be interested in.'

His gaze levelled with hers. 'Then why are you blushing, Kate?'

Scarlet-faced, she began to pack away several bottles and items of equipment, conscious of his gaze fixed on her as he controlled his laughter. 'If you must know, they seem to think you . . . and I . . . that we . . .' she licked her dry lips '. . . that we'd have lots of beautiful babies.'

'It's an interesting theory,' he drawled softly.

'Well, I suggest you put them right on the subject,' she flung at him.

'Why should I spoil their fun?'

She took a deep breath, knowing that words would choke her. Suddenly the thought of having babies—Jake Ramsey's babies—filled her with a kind of longing she had never thought possible. With a quick movement she turned away. 'The patients are waiting, Doctor. Shall we get started?'

'Most of these people look remarkably healthy to me.'

'They probably are,' she agreed wryly. 'We can usually count on a good turnout. Unless something really urgent crops up, most patients wait until we pay a visit rather than come to the hospital.' She gave him a look. 'This is a little unusual. We get so few strangers here, a certain amount of curiosity is inevitable.'

'In that case perhaps I'd better make myself useful and do something to satisfy their curiosity.' A nerve pulsed in his jaw. 'Tell me which patients you'd like me to see.'

'I didn't mean——' she began, but he cut across her.

'I know that. You don't need to be so defensive.'

Kate clenched her teeth, thinking that she could never be anything else when he was around. 'I just didn't want you to imagine I was trying to . . . to prove some kind of point, that's all.'

'And were you?'

'No, of course not. You don't *seriously* imagine I could have planned all this?'

'The thought did occur to me.'

Kate felt her cheeks flush with colour. 'I didn't know we were going to hold a clinic today, if you remember?'

He seemed to take stock of her, the unwittingly defensive stance of her slim figure, the lift to her chin, and she found the experience highly disconcerting. 'Well, since I am here, shouldn't we stop wasting time, and get on with the job in hand?'

Kate could only seethe inwardly as he settled himself on one of the canvas chairs, and beckoned the first patient forward. It would jolly well serve him right if they refused, she thought ungraciously, and suffered the galling ignominy of watching a queue form rapidly in front of his own table, while she had to entice her own patient out from behind his mother's skirts with a bribe in the form of a bag of sweets.

They worked in comparative silence, both concentrating on their individual patients, most of whom she had come to know personally in the weeks since her arrival on the island.

One elderly man had been receiving regular

treatment for an eye condition. It was a particularly distressing complaint, transmitted not only by flies but by worms too. She couldn't help feeling a pang of sympathy for the man as he sat quietly while she changed the dressings. She was reaching for a pair of scissors when Jake spoke.

'Do you mind if I take a look?'

'Why, no, of course not.' She moved aside. 'I'd be grateful for a second opinion.'

He leaned forward, and began gently to question the man, carrying out his own brief examination before turning to her again. 'How many cases of eye disease do you see out here?'

'Too many.' Her reply was unequivocal. 'We need more drugs, more preventive medicines, but, in the last resort, what we most desperately need is the means to carry out minor surgery, which could probably save the sight of a lot of these people.'

Jake cut across again. 'You don't have to sell your case to me. I've seen symptoms and conditions like these all over the world. They all need precisely what you're asking for, but it's never that simple.'

'You're saying it's a matter of priorities, is that it?' Her cheeks were flushed with indignation. 'Basic finance. It comes down to that? Someone sits in a fancy office, deciding who gets the miracle this year?'

'Don't be so bloody naïve,' he grated. 'There aren't any miracles, and it isn't all down to money though, God knows, it helps. It's down to people

as well, and overcoming their natural fears and
ignorance, but it won't happen overnight, maybe
not in the next decade—who knows?—maybe not
in my lifetime, but do you think I don't care, or
feel, just as deeply as you do?'

Kate swallowed the sudden tightness in her
throat. 'I . . . I'm sorry.'

'No.' For an instant their eyes met and held. 'I'm
sorry.' A derisive smile lifted the corners of his
mouth.

'But you were right,' she said hastily. 'It was
wrong of me to make judgements on a subject I
know very little about.'

In face, she knew very little about Jake Ramsey.
She was torn between resentment of what he
represented, and a reluctant yet compelling
attraction to him. He seemed capable of arousing
all kinds of new and frightening emotions within
her, emotions which left her feeling excited, yet
confused. Jake Ramsey was unlike any other man
she had known before.

He was also a brilliantly competent doctor.
More than an hour later, having watched him
work, she had accepted that fact. He seemed to
have a natural affinity with the people whom he
was treating. Even when Kate was certain that he
must suspect there was no physical basis for a
consultation, but only sheer curiosity, he listened
patiently.

She flexed her shoulders and arms wearily,

trying to ignore the incessant throbbing of taut muscles as she dusted an open wound with antibiotic powder, before reaching for a supply of tablets from her bag. She shook several into a container. 'Take one of these twice a day, Seni. Sun up and sun down,' she explained carefully. 'They will help prevent any infection. And try to keep a clean dressing on that foot, so it will heal faster.'

Jake was completing an examination as she looked up from writing her notes. She hadn't noticed before quite how thick his dark hair was, or how surprisingly gentle those strong hands could be. She told herself her interest was strickly that of one professional for another. His total absorption in what he was doing gave her an opportunity to observe him for several minutes, without his actually being aware of it. Or at least that was what she imagined, until he turned to stare with cool deliberation, directly into her eyes, a faint smile on his lips.

'Interested?'

She drew back, feeling the colour surge into her cheeks. 'Not in the least!'

'Pity,' he said smoothly. 'Ophthalmics is a fascinating subject.'

She made a slight choking sound and his eyebrows rose. 'What did you think I meant, Kate?'

She wasn't fooled for one moment by his bland expression. He knew exactly what she had been thinking. Kate slapped a pair of scissors into his hand so that he could complete a clean dressing. 'I'd forgotten that ophthalmics is your speciality, that's all.'

'Used to be,' he corrected mildly.

'Surely you must have some regrets?' she asked. 'Giving up everything you had for this . . .'

He didn't look up, but she sensed a sudden tension in him. 'My life suits me the way it is. When it doesn't, I'll move on, but there's nothing I'd ever want to go back to. Does that answer your question?'

His voice was perfectly controlled, but she sensed that she had somehow touched a raw nerve. The intensity of his response had surprised her and she began to realise that she knew nothing at all about Jake Ramsey and the emotions which governed him.

Tight-lipped, Kate forced her attention back to her work, reminding herself that his private life was none of her concern. He had made that very clear. But her hands were still shaking as she packed away a box of syringes and waited for her next patient, all the time very much aware of the man beside her.

She pushed a strand of hair from her eyes, feeling dust and perspiration on her skin. The thought of standing under a cold shower or stripping off her clothes and plunging into the lagoon rose tantalisingly in her mind, only to be pushed away as she became aware of him watching her.

With a quick movement she turned away, forcing her attention back to her work. The sun was at its hottest when she straightened up again, passing her parched tongue over dry lips. Jake seemed impervious to the heat. He worked like a machine, she thought, except that she knew he wasn't. The lines of tension had gone from his face, leaving it relaxed, and so gentle as he spoke soothingly to a child that her heart gave an odd little lurch in her breast.

The ground seemed to shift suddenly beneath her feet and she swayed slightly, pressing a hand to her eyes.

Jake looked up sharply. 'Are you all right?'

'Fine.' With a quick movement she turned away, licking her dry lips. Her hands were shaking as she reached for a fresh needle and began drawing up the next vaccine. To her dismay it fell to the floor. Tight-lipped, she reached for another, aware of the ridiculous tears stinging at her lashes. What on earth was the matter with her?

Jake's hand came down on her arm. He said something to the woman who smiled and sat patiently as he drew Kate away from the table into the shade, where she closed her eyes and stood breathing deeply.

'Why don't you take a break?' His gaze was penetrating and she despised herself for letting him see her weakness. 'There's a flask of juice in the back of the Land Rover.'

Kate shook her head, and wished she hadn't as the wave of dizziness returned in full force. 'I'm sorry. I don't know what's happening. I'm not usually the fainting sort.' She felt hot and exhausted, and ran the back of her hand over her forehead as she straightened up. 'I'll be all right. I need a fresh batch of syringes.'

'That can wait.' His mouth tightened. 'We could both do with a drink. We can finish later.'

'Really, there's no need . . .'

'I'd say there's every need. You've been working at full stretch for weeks, and you're still not properly acclimatised to this heat.' His voice was surprisingly concerned. 'It's my fault for not insisting that you take a few days off.'

'There's no need for that.' Her lips trembled. 'I'm perfectly capable of carrying on. Besides, I'd rather. The sooner we get finished, the sooner we can get back.'

Humour glinted briefly in his eyes. 'And the sooner you get away from me, it that it?'

'You said it.'

For a second his eyes widened, then it was as if a shutter came down. 'If you're worried about the boyfriend, don't be. I'm sure he'll wait.'

It was her turn to be confused, then realisation dawned. He was talking about Nori! 'As a matter of fact, that wasn't what I meant. I don't like being away from the hospital too long.'

'I'm glad to hear it.' His mouth tightened. 'I wouldn't advise you to become too involved when your stay here is going to be limited. Or hadn't you thought of that?' he said grimly.

Kate was shocked by the trace of anger in his voice. She stared at him, unable to stem the tide of angry colour which flooded her face and throat. 'I'll bear it in mind.'

'Do that,' he snapped, 'because I certainly have no intention of sticking around to tidy up any loose ends after you've gone.'

He turned and strode away, leaving her staring after him. She felt totally bewildered by what seemed a completely unjustified attack. What could have prompted it? Professional seniority didn't give him the right to pass judgement on her private life, yet what else could it be? Kate shook her head. The idea that a man like Jake Ramsey could be jealous of Nori was ludicrous. So what . . .?

Sighing, she gave up and went back to work, refusing to look at him again until the last patient had gone, then she automatically began to clear the equipment away. Collecting syringes and dressings, she counted the number of vaccines used, packing everything away into containers.

She paused to brush a hand wearily through her hair. She felt drained and in need of that drink. Jake could make his own way back to the Land Rover.

Back at the vehicle, Kate helped herself to some

juice from the vacuum flask, letting the ice-cold liquid trickle slowly down her throat. The relief it brought was sheer bliss, as she sat with her eyes closed, letting her head rest against the back of the seat.

Gradually a feeling of lethargy began to steal over her. She didn't want to fight with Jake, wasn't even sure why it had started, except that it hadn't been her fault. She had simply retaliated. But that was the kind of effect he had on her. Jake Ramsey wasn't the sort of man you could ignore. He set waves in motion, and before you knew it you were being swept along, caught up in currents too stong to fight.

Kate sipped some more of the juice from the cup and let her eyes drift shut again. Curiosity about his private life got the better of her. She had definitely touched upon a raw nerve when she had suggested that he must miss life back home. Something—or someone—had obviously made him bitter. A woman . . . or a wife!

Kate didn't know why the thought had only just occurred to her. She might have known that a man like Jake had to be married, or have a woman somewhere in his life, but for some reason she felt suddenly cold and miserable. The idea that she was actually jealous hit her like a physical blow which left her shaking. It was ridiculous, she told herself. But the memory of a fleeting moment spent in his arms, and a kiss which had set her senses reeling, kept coming back to taunt her with the inescapable thought that she had enjoyed the experience!

'I hope you left some of that for me.'

At the sound of Jake's deep voice, her eyes flew open and she jerked forward, spilling juice on her shirt. 'Damn! Did you have to creep up on me like that? Now look what you've made me do.' Brushing furiously at the stain, she found that the idea that he had been standing there, watching her, was vastly disturbing.

'I didn't creep,' he replied calmly, flinging his bag into the back of the Land Rover. 'You were asleep, otherwise you would have heard me.'

'Nonsense. I had my eyes closed, that's all.'

'Funny, I could have sworn you were dreaming. Disturbing dreams, too, if your expressions were anything to go by. I was debating whether to leave you to it, but I needed that drink too much.'

'So greed won out on chivalry. Here.' She handed him the flask. 'There's plenty.'

He filled the cup, draining it in one go. 'In that case you'd better have some more.'

'No, thanks. I don't need it.'

Jake's hand shot out to cover hers. 'It's not chivalry, just common sense. You've lost a lot of fluid. We both have. Dehydration makes you snappy—or hadn't you noticed?'

'In that case, you'd better have the lot,' she smiled sweetly, 'since your need is obviously far greater than mine.' She had half turned away when his grip on her arm jerked her back.

'Take it,' he repeated, 'or I'll force it down your throat.'

Her eyes widened. She didn't doubt for one minute that he meant it. Her hands tightened furiously on the cup. Jake moved a step closer. 'Drink it.'

She swallowed convulsively, forcing the sticky liquid down her throat. It was blissfully cool and refreshing and she had to prevent herself from licking her lips. 'Satisfied?' Ungraciously she thrust the cup at him. 'Your turn, I think.'

He took the cup, screwing it back on to the flask. 'Thanks, but I'm not thirsty.'

Kate faced him, her eyes stormy as angry disbelief tightened her deicate features. 'Well, of all the . . . I suppose you get some sort of kick out of displaying your male physical superiority, it that it?' She caught the faint hint of mockery in his eyes and knew that he was deliberately baiting her.

'If that was what I had in mind, I'm sure I could think of far better ways.'

Blue eyes met hers, and Kate swallowed the sudden tightness in her throat as he began to unfasten his shirt.

'Wh . . . what are you doing?'

'What does it look like?' His face remained implacable as he peeled off the shirt, exposing the sheer, physical perfection of his hard-muscled chest and powerful shoulders.

Kate felt her body quiver with awareness. She tried to tear her gaze away, but couldn't. He said something, but his voice was muffled, lost beneath the frantic thudding of her own heartbeats. Something very strange was happening to her. She wanted to run, to escape from the tide of emotions welling up and threatening to consume her, but she couldn't move, dared not move, for fear of betraying her thoughts to this man.

She realised that he was speaking. Her eyes flew open. 'Wh . . . what?' She gazed into his taut features.

'I said take this.'

She stared at the T-shirt, her fingers closing numbly over the fabric. 'Why?'

His eyebrows rose. 'It may not be the right size, but I'm sure you can improvise. Knot the ends, or something.'

Kate jerked back to reality in a torment of shame, to see Jake shrugging himself into a clean shirt. Hot-cheeked, she thrust the T-shirt back at him. 'No, thanks, I'll manage.'

He shot her a mocking glance. 'If it's your modesty you're worried about, you can always get changed on the other side of the vehicle.'

Kate flushed at the vein of sarcasm in his voice. It was half in her mind to stick to her guns and refuse, but her sweat-soaked shirt felt as if it were moulded to her body, revealing every contour.

'Thanks. I'll be as quick as I can.'

'Take your time, I'll stow the equipment.'

'Mr Efficient,' Kate muttered between her teeth, as she scuttled behind the Land Rover and began tugging at her shirt buttons. 'Yes, sir. No, sir. Three bags full, sir.'

'Did you say something?'

'Not a thing. Damn!' She swore softly as a fingernail broke.

'Be sure and call if you need any help.'

Like hell. Kate's hands shook with sudden nervousness. Slipping out of her shirt, she fumbled her way into the T-shirt, cursing softly as the voluminous folds caught in her hair, loosening it from its clips and jerking painfully at her scalp. In sudden panic she fought her way upwards through the suffocating layer, to emerge, breathing hard, hair in disarray.

Heart thudding, she swept it aside, gazing down with dismay at the T-shirt. It hung loosely, leaving her breasts exposed. Her mouth trembled. 'Oh, great. Miss Great Britain wins the booby prize.' Jake Ramsey's chest measurements obviously bore no relation to her own.

'Are you nearly ready?'

She clutched the tent-like garment to her. How she hated Jake Ramsey. 'Give me two minutes,' she choked. Improvise, improvise. With what? an inner voice demanded hysterically. She reached for the cast-off shirt. It was damp with sweat and adhering sand and sticky orange stain. 'Yeuk!'

She concentrated her efforts on the T-shirt, hauling it upwards until it covered her breasts. Great. What to do with six inches of excess shoulder strap. Knit yourself a knot.

With trembling fingers she twisted one strap securely into place and began to struggle with the other. The sound of a sudden movement at the rear end of the Land Rover made her clumsy. As her arm jerked up, her elbow caught a glancing blow against the door of the vehicle, sending pain and numbness shooting through her arm. Gasping with shock, she clung to the door in an attempt to steady herself as a wave of nausea threatened to engulf her. Kate made a feeble attempt to cover her semi-nakedness as Jake's footsteps approached.

'Are you all right back there?'

She swallowed convulsively. Her skin felt dotted with perspiration, and she rested her head briefly against her arm, pleading silently with him to go away. Oh, God, the nausea rose in her throat.

Kate froze as Jake's hands caught at her shoulders. She tried to resist, but he was too strong and she turned to face him, tears of pain and vexation welling up in her eyes.

She saw his eyes widen briefly. He swore softly under his breath, then she was in his arms. The sheer, physical impact as their bodies made contact was like nothing she had experienced before. She could hear the quickening beat of his heart as she leaned against him. The raw build-up of nervous tension came to a head and the floodgates finally gave way. She didn't know why she wept. She was only aware of his hands, gently cupping her face, brushing away a strand of hair. There was a brief moment of hesitation in his eyes before his head moved, and his mouth came down on hers in a kiss so gentle, as it seemed to search and question, that, almost without knowing how it happened, she wrapped her arms round his neck and gave her mouth up to his.

Kate closed her eyes, surrendering herself completely to the gentle, but increasing pressure of his lips against hers. She knew that he wanted her. A shock wave of desire rippled down her spine. Then, suddenly, without any warning, she felt a shudder run through him. His body tensed and he released her.

Kate looked up, startled. She caught a brief moment of unguarded vulnerability on his face that took her so completely by surprise that she told herself she must have imagined it. Her eyelids felt heavy, as if she had woken from a drugged sleep. She pressed a hand to her mouth, her emotions raw and tingling from the encounter, and it came as a shock to realise that he was looking at her with a wary kind of confusion in his eyes.

'We'd better get back,' he said abruptly.

Just like that, she thought, swallowing the tight knot of misery in her throat as she struggled to gather the remaining shreds of her dignity. Hadn't that kiss meant anything at all to him?

Obviously not, she decided, as he climbed into the Land Rover beside her and started the engine. He couldn't wait to get back to the hospital. As far as Jake Ramsey was concerned, it was a case of out of sight, out of mind. She turned to stare unseeingly out of the window, rather than let him see the confusion and embarrassment in her eyes.

This is ridiculous, she told herself, blinking against the tears that blurred her vision. But, ridiculous or not, it didn't explain why she should feel so cheated.

CHAPTER SIX

ALTHOUGH she hadn't expected to, Kate slept soundly for the first time in months. So soundly, in fact, that one morning, a few days later, she woke to discover that the alarm clock had apparently rung itself to a standstill without her even hearing it. She hadn't even stirred when Selena had brought in the tray of tea which stood, cold and untouched, on the bedside table.

What finally penetrated her state of semiconsciousness was the sound of a bell, and it definitely was not of the alarm variety, except inasmuch as it sent some vague signal of warning to her sleep-clogged brain.

Groaning into her pillow, Kate stirred, opened one eye to glare at the clock and, in a panic, leapt out of bed. Nine o'clock! She should have been on duty an hour ago. Jake Ramsey was going to have a field day.

Grabbing her thin cotton robe, she headed for the shower. It wasn't until she was standing beneath the tepid water, letting it trickle through her hair, that she remembered that today was Sunday!

'Idiot!' she told her reflection fiercely as she lathered her body, revelling in the momentary bliss of the cool water. But at least by the time she had dried herself, given a light dusting of powder over her skin and slipped into fresh undies, she was feeling decidedly more human.

Sunday was the one day of the week when there was no clinic, and, in common with most of the islanders, Kate made her way to the tiny church, where she sat in one of the pews and listened with infinite pleasure to the sound of familiar, old hymns, sung in the hauntingly beautiful and melodic rhythm of the islands.

It didn't even seem to matter that there wasn't always a preacher. Visiting missionaries sometimes came, but the last permanent priest had died only weeks before her own arrival and a replacement hadn't yet arrived, so the villagers improvised by singing more lustily than ever and Nori read the lesson.

Once or twice, as she sat, letting the sounds drift over her, she felt her gaze straying, surveying the rows of faces, curious to see whether Jake would be drawn to put in an appearance, but he didn't.

Nor was he in evidence later, when she went to do an afternoon in-patient round at the hospital. Indeed she had hardly even seen him since they'd held the joint clinic. It occurred to her that perhaps he was deliberately avoiding her. Kate felt the muscles in her throat tighten. She could have saved him the trouble. After their last encounter she wasn't exactly looking forward to seeing him again either. But it didn't stop her heart thudding every time a figure appeared through the swing doors.

Slipping into her white coat, she headed for her father's room. To her surprise it was empty. David Sulo, one of the orderlies, answered her silent query. 'He's sitting out on the veranda, Doctor. I wheeled him there myself about half an hour ago.'

Kate nodded her thanks and went out to where a figure sat, a closed book lying on the table beside him.

'Dad?'

John Tyson gave a slight start, half turning at the sound of her voice. 'Kate! I didn't hear you.'

'I'm not surprised. You were miles away.' She bent to kiss him. 'What are you doing, sitting out here alone?'

'Dreaming.' He patted her cheek and waved her to a chair. 'I do it best out here on my own. I listen to the sea and smell the air. Have you noticed how scents are exaggerated at night, when the air cools?'

She lifted her gaze to follow his and her throat tighten. 'O, Dad. I know how much you're going to miss all this. I just wish . . . I wish there was something . . .'

His hand came out quickly to grasp hers. 'You mustn't feel that way.'

'But it's so unfair. All you need is time to get some of your strength back again'.

'I'm feeling much better. The truth is, I'm just

enjoying being lazy.'

She went along with that pretence as she leaned forward to pour him a drink from the jug on the table, painfully conscious that he seemed to be fighting for breath. 'Why don't you apply for some home leave? You're long overdue. You could take six months back in England, then come back . . .'

'It's a nice thought, darling.' He smiled. 'But I'm not sure it's what I want. These past weeks have given me time to think, if nothing else. Perhaps it's time I took another look at my life.'

She swallowed her own drink, and got to her feet. 'But I thought this was what you wanted. After Mother died——'

'After your mother died things were very different. It took me a long time to come to terms with my life without her. I can't pretend it will ever be the same, but it's true that time does take the edge off grief.' He watched her as she brushed a strand of hair from her eyes. 'I think it's time to let someone younger and fitter take over.'

'How can you say that? You're still young, and you've done so much out here.'

John Tyson laughed softly. 'Then maybe it's time someone else took a share.' Suddenly his grey eyes were serious. 'Don't worry about me, darling. I'm perfectly all right.'

Kate directed her attention purposely away from the lines of tiredness in his face. 'Are you really, though?' she asked gently.

He patted her hand, then let it go.'Be a good girl, don't fuss.'

She had to swallow hard on all the arguments which rose to her lips. Instead, she set her glass down and glanced at her watch. 'All right, I won't. For the moment you can consider yourself let off the hook. I have to go and do my round anyway.'

'You like the work, don't you?'

'Oh, yes, I love it. I love the island. I can understand how you feel about it.'

'How about Jake? How do you two get on together?'

She bit her lip. 'I really don't know him that well. He's brilliant doctor . . .'

'But?'

She didn't question his assumption that there was a but. He knew her too well. Her hand moved in a restless gesture. 'I don't think I know him well enough to make a judgement on him as a man. It's just that, well, every time we meet we seem to strike sparks off each other.'

'Mm. That's odd. I always found him very easy to get on with.' The grey eyes look at her shrewdly. 'Perhaps when you get to know him better——'

'I won't be here long enough,'Kate reminded him, bending to kiss his cheek again. And even given all the time in the world, she thought, as she made her way to the wards, she wasn't sure that she would ever understand Jake Ramsey. It was as if he had raised some kind of invisible barrier between himself and the world, and it had been lowered, only briefly, but long enough for her to glimpse something of the man beyond. A strangely contradictory man, a mixture of compassion and arrogance, and she knew quite well which emotion he saved for herself.

Maggie was busy shaking down a thermometer when Kate entered the unit. She made a careful note of the reading before looking up, her eyes troubled above the surgical mask she was wearing.

'I thought you'd want to see the latest admission as soon as possible. He was brought in about an hour ago, suffering from head injuries.'

'Any idea of the cause?'

Maggie shook her head. 'We're still trying to find out, but the most urgent priority was to try and get him stabilised.'

'You did the right thing.' Kate was already reaching for a stethoscope as she bent to look at the man lying on the bed. He was about forty. His eyes were closed, and his skin had the clammy feel, indicative of a patient in deep shock. 'Has there been any change at all since he was brought in?'

'Only very slight.' Maggie took an ophthalmoscope from the nearby trolley, anticipating its need. 'He opened his eyes just for a few seconds, tried to speak, then went out like a light again.'

'Well, at least that's a reasonably good sign.' Kate felt a tiny spasm of relief. 'Any indication that he recognised you or knew where he was?'

'None, but there wasn't time.'

'Mm,' Kate frowned. 'I'd be more worried if he hadn't regained consciousness at all.' she felt for the pulse. It was shallow but even. Taking the ophthalmoscope, she spent several minutes searching for the tell-tale signs of injury before straightening up. 'Well, there's definitely a severe concussion. I'll need to look at the X-rays before I can dismiss the possibility of a skull fracture, though I'd say it's not likely.' She leaned closer to peer at the wound on the side of the man's neck as Maggie swabbed the area with antiseptic. 'That's not too bad. It looks worse than it is. It'll need a few stitches, but I don't think it will give us any problems. Has he vomited?'

'Yes, as he was being admitted. Not since.'

Kate nodded, then she bent to sturdy the man again, easing his mouth slightly open. She straightened up, frowning.

'Something wrong?'

'I'm not certain. Just a suspicion. Have you taken any urine samples yet?'

'No, there hasn't been time. Why, do you want one?'

'Yes, please, and make it urgent, will you? Have we any previous records for this particular patient?'

'None that I've been able to trace, but Benjamin is going through the files.' Maggie looked at her. 'What do you think?'

'I'm not sure.' Kate brushed her hand against the man's skin, gently pinching it between her fingers. 'He's very dehydrated, and I think there's a smell of ketones on his breath. I'm wondering whether we might have a case of diabetes here. The head injuries could be incidental, a result of the fall when he collapsed.'

'I'll get on to it straight away. What about medication?'

'Let's find out what we're dealing with first. I'll write up some pain-killers. He's going to have a king-sized headache when he wakes up. Apart from that, complete, rest, no movement, no noise. Keep the room dark. That should take care of the concussion. We'll deal with the diabetes as soon as I get that urine sample and confirm that that's what we're dealing with.'

'I'll scc to it.' Maggie wrote a rapid series of notes, and slipped her pen into the pocket of her dress.'Where are you off to now?'

'Mums and babies,'

'Have you been in to see your dad?'

'Mm, a while ago.'

'How is he?'

Kate sighed. 'A bit low.'

'That could be the medication.'

'I know. That's what I keep telling myself

but . . .' Kate shrugged. 'Oh, I don't know. Perhaps I'm worrying unnecessarily. I just wish I could get to the bottom of whatever it is that's troubling him, that's all. It's almost as if he's giving in.'

Maggie nodded sympathetically. 'Have you had a chat with Dr Ramsey? He's been spending quite a bit of time with your dad lately. They seem to get on well together.'

'That only makes it worse. Why isn't Dad fighting against being sent home? It isn't like him to give in so easily. It can only be because he's being taken in by the Ramsey charm.'

'Oh, you admit he has charm then?' Maggie's eyes sparkled with humour. 'Look, I hate to say this, but has it occurred to you that you could be overlooking one real possibility?'

'What do you mean?'

'Well, simply that your dad may actually want to go home? Perhaps he feels he's done all he can out here. He may just have had enough.'

Kate stared at her, then shook her head. 'I don't believe it. Dad loves this place too much.'

Maggie shrugged. 'It was just an idea.'

'I appreciate your concern, but until recently, Dad was still talking about how much he still wanted to do. It doesn't add up, unless there's something he's not telling me.' Kate picked up a batch of case notes. 'Look, I'd better go. The patients tend to become slightly aggressive if I disturb their afternoon tea. Let me have the results of that urine test as soon as you can.'

'Will do.'

Kate paused on her way to the ward to check the contents of the drugs cupboard, and was frowning over the dwindling stock of supplies when a voice came from behind her.

'It's not so good. Better chase order, or we run out altogether.'

'Sue Ling!' Kate whirled round to confront the petite young Chinese girl, who returned her smile. 'You're back!'

'Today first time.'

'But are you better?'

The slender figure in the short-sleeved white dress chuckled.

'Spots all gone. Besides, how can you run this place without me? I decided time I get back to work.'

'Well, I'm delighted, and there's certainly plenty of work to do.'

'So I see.' Sue Ling led the way towards the children's ward, her pretty face, with its high cheekbones and vivacious brown eyes, framed by short, jet-black hair. 'I've been getting to know my new patients, and a noisy lot they are, too.' She waved a greeting to the children, and they shouted back, delighted. One of them, who couldn't have been more than four years old, came to clutch at her hand. 'This young lady tells me her name is

Safaia, and she has leg go sick.' Behind the smile her gaze went questioningly to Kate.

She nodded. 'I suppose that's one way of putting it. Safaia was born with a congenital dislocation of the hip, which, with proper medical care, would have been treated the moment it was diagnosed. In Safaia's case the condition went undiagnosed, simply because no medical advice was available at birth. Her parents simply assumed that because she was born with some apparent defect, it was the fault of the spirits and something they had to accept.'

'But how could she get about?'

'Apparently they made her some kind of cart. The other children used to pull her around after them. Until we spotted the problem, and managed to persuade Safaia's parents to let us send Safaia over to the hospital on the big island for corrective surgery. She's just got back.'

Sue Ling smiled. 'Well, she certainly looks fine now.'

'She is, except that we have to make sure she gets regular physiotherapy.'

They watched the child go off happily to join her companions, before Kate said softly, 'Getting her parents to accept her back again will be the biggest problem, unfortunately.'

Sue Ling stared at her. 'You mean they reject her?'

'I'm afraid it sometimes happens. Fortunately,

it's rare out here, but there are still a few islanders who believe far more strongly in the spirits than they do in modern science.'

'But that is awful.'

'Yes, it is. Ironic, too, when there are people like Joanna, who desperately want a child, yet here she is, grieving over a second miscarriage.'

'How is she today?'

'Actually, a little brighter.' Sue Ling handed her the case notes.' I've noticed she has begun to take some of the smaller children under her wing.'

'Oh, that's marvellous. It may be just what she needs.'

'I think so. I watch but say nothing. Best she thinks we don't notice.'

'Let's go and take a look at the mums and ladies-in-waiting.' Kate walked into the small unit reserved for maternity cases. Only one bed was in use and that was occupied by a very young, heavily pregnant girl who lay with her hands gripping the sheet, groaning softly as she twisted her head from side to side. A nearby fan wafted the air, not very effectively, and her skin was dotted with perspiration. She saw Kate, and reached out to grip her hand.

Kate smiled reassuringly, turning briefly from the bed to don the gown and mask Sue Ling held out for her. In a low voice she said urgently, 'How old is the patient? She looks scarcely more than a child herself.'

The Chinese girl met Kate's gaze above her mask. 'She says fifteen. My guess would be nearer fourteen.'

'I think you may be right.'

'Baby come soon.' The grunted words were almost a plea rather than a question as another contraction distorted the girl's features.

Placing a hand gently on the hardening abdomen, Kate waited, feeling the strength of the contraction as it built up to a peak before fading again. 'She's getting some very strong contractions. They're lasting too. How long has she been in labour?'

'I guess many hours before mother bring her in.' Sue Ling began to bathe the girl's hot face with a sponge.

Kate straightened up after making a gentle but thorough examination. 'Yes, so would I. It's taking too long. I'm afraid either her pelvis is too narrow, preventing the baby from dropping down, or it could be lying in a breech position. I'll need to do a proper examination, but either way she's going to need help, and soon, if we're not going to end up losing the mother and the baby.'

She had moved away from the bed, dropping her voice. 'Why, in heaven's name, did they leave it so long before bringing her in! The girl herself isn't very strong.'

'Is anything wrong?'

Kate's heart gave a traitorous thud as she turned

to stare into Jake's calm, rugged features. She told herself it was simple relief at seeing him standing there, which sent the ridiculous jolt of pleasure running through her. After their earlier encounter, it certainly couldn't be anything else, yet for some reason she was glad of the mask which hid most of her face.

'We have a patient in labour. She's very young. We think probably no more than fourteen. It's a first baby, obviously full term and quite big.'

Jake nodded. 'So what's the problem, apart from the mother's age?'

'From external examination, I think there's a chance it may be a breech, and her pelvis is very narrow.'

'Would you like me to take a look?'

Kate shot him a swift look of gratitude. 'Would you? I don't think we have much time to lose. The mother's blood pressure is starting to give some cause for concern.'

'Just give me a few minutes to scrub up.'

Gowned and masked, Jake's examination of the girl confirmed their worst fears. 'You're right,' he said grimly at last, stripping off the surgical gloves. 'She's never to going to make it on her own. The baby's tucked in at an angle. We're going to have to do something pretty fast.'

Kate tugged down her own mask. You mean a caesarian?'

'There's no other choice,' Jake said, giving her a

straight look. 'The mother is already exhausted. If we do nothing, we could lose both.'

Kate knew that he was right, but, looking around the tiny and sparsely equipped unit, she felt herself battling with a sense of panic. 'Have you ever performed a caesarian?'

'Not routinely, no, I must admit, but I am a surgeon and, right now, I don't see any alternative, do you?'

'You realise we don't have the proper facilities?'

'Then we'll have to improvise,' he said evenly. 'It's been done before, Kate. We can rig up lights, using the generator. Scrub up the largest table we can find.'

Sue Ling looked from one to the other. 'I see to it now.' She bustled out, already beckoning to one of the orderlies and issuing commands.

Jake's blue eyes met and held Kate's, almost as if he sensed the turmoil she was feeling, then he reached out, taking one of her hands in his, squeezing gently. 'I'm going to need your help, Kate.'

Something in his voice seemed to penetrate her brain, having a strangely calming effect. She looked up at him and nodded shakily. 'I'm sorry, but this is all a bit new to me. I'm afraid you're going to have to tell me what to do.'

His mouth twisted slightly. 'It's new to me, too,' he said softly. 'So it rather looks as if we're going to have to help one another. Ready?'

She drew a deep breath. 'Tell me what you need.'

'Good girl.'

For some ridiculous reason, those two quietly spoken words seemed to give her all the confidence she needed.

In the event, it was all over amazingly quickly. Almost before she realised it, she was helping to lift out the squirming scrap of life, seeing its tiny fists instinctively go to its mouth where it began to suck noisily. Nature's most primeval response was at work. Only a few seconds after birth, and a healthy baby was hungry!

Kate looked up to find Jake watching her, a curiously gentle expression in the blue eyes which told her that he shared at least something of what she was feeling. Blushing, she turned away, wrapping the infant in a blanket before handing it to Sue Ling.

The rest of the procedure was routine. It was only later, when the patient was sleeping peacefully with the baby beside her, that Kate finally had time to draw breath and reflect on what had taken place. She felt drained, both physically and mentally, yet, at the same time, intensely satisfied. She had played some minor part in a miracle, and that image of the mother and child would stay with her for a very long time.

Darkness had fallen by the time she was ready to leave the hospital to walk back to her bungalow. The last time she had seen Jake he had been making a last check on the mother and baby, so it came as a surprise to see him walking along the path to join her.

As he came towards her out of the darkness, she was hit again by the feeling of physical attraction she always experienced whenever he came near, and knew too that it was something she must fight. Simply because—the thought hit her like a cold wave—she was in love with Jake Ramsey. She drew in a swift breath, shaken by the admission, her face suddenly pale. It was true, no matter how much she might try to deny it, just as it was also true that there was no future in it. The fact that he had kissed her merely proved that he found her physically attractive. It didn't mean he was looking for a deep relationship. That much had been made very clear when he had released her so abruptly the moment she had let herself respond. Almost as if he had been afraid that she might read more into it than he had been prepared to give.

She blinked the tears furiously from her eyes. 'How are the patients?'

'Sleeping peacefully. Mother and baby both doing well.'

'Thanks to you.' Her voice came out thickly and Jake came to a halt in front of her, his hands coming to rest on her shoulders. 'I seem to remember that you did your share. I certainly couldn't have done it without you.'

She was tense with the need to resist the

powerful feelings he was evoking. 'Oh, I'm sure you would have managed, somehow.' Her throat was dry with panic. 'I would have lost them both.'

'Hey!' His hand was suddenly under her chin, tilting her face up. 'What's this? Surely not tears? But why?'

Kate sniffed hard. The obvious assumption was the safest one. 'Reaction, I should think. I've never had a baby by caesarian before.'

'I'm pretty new at it myself.' He cleared his throat as if it were suddenly troubling him. 'Look, I give you my word, the baby may be a bit on the small side, but she's going to thrive thanks to some fine team work.'

Salt seeped deeper into the wound! They stood in the darkness, listening to the distant sound of surf. Neither of them seemed to want to move.

Kate broke the silence first. 'I'm glad they're going to be OK.'

'So am I.' He seemed to sigh; then, with a jerky movement, he straightened. 'You'd better get some sleep. It's been a long day.'

He was doing it again, dismissing her, as if she were some kind of irritation he had to be rid of. He was leaning against the wall, not looking at her.

'I suppose it has been, for both of us. But what about you?'

'There are still things I have to do.'

'Can't they wait?'

He seemed to tense for a moment before he turned to stare at her. Almost hesitantly he held out of his hand, and she took it. Before she knew it, she was in his arms, her body pressed against his, her heart beating faster as his mouth came down over hers.

How long the kiss lasted, who broke away first, she couldn't have said. They parted, breathless, and she stared at him, wondering at the expression she saw in his eyes.

'You'd better go,' he rasped.

She didn't want to go. She wanted to stay, to hold on to that feeling of excitement and fierce desire she knew had been entirely mutual. His hands cupped her face as if he sensed the question that must be mirrored so starkly in her eyes. Then he broke the contact, lifting his head slowly, and before she could speak he had turned and was striding away.

Kate stood watching before making her own way to the bungalow, but when she turned, unable to resist one last look, he was standing gazing out towards the lagoon, until, as if coming to a sudden decision, he bent to pick up a pebble, and aimed it viciously into the surf before turning on his heel and walking back along the path to the hospital.

CHAPTER SEVEN

'GONE! Kate felt her mouth become suddenly very dry. 'I don't understand. What do you mean, he's gone?'

Maggie frowned. 'Dr Ramsey left yesterday. But I thought you knew.'

Kate stared at her, tight-lipped, and shook her head. 'No, I had no idea.'

Maggie put down the cards she had been sorting. 'He came in early, apparently expecting to find you here. I explained that it was your day off and that you'd planned to go to the reef, but that I could get a message to you later, when you came in to do a round.' Her brow furrowed. 'He seemed a bit put out, but said not to disturb you, but I assumed he must have discussed it with you, or at least left a message.'

Kate swallowed hard. 'No, he didn't. Not a word.'

'Well, I must say, it does seem a bit odd.'

'Did . . . did he say where he was going? Or for how long?'

'I gathered he had some urgent cables to send and some arrangements to make. He wasn't particularly forthcoming on either. He asked one of the men to take him by canoe, over to the big island.'

Kate listened in silence, feeling the colour drain from her face. 'Did he say when he . . . If he intends coming back?'

Maggie shook her head. 'That's the odd thing. Not a word. But he wouldn't just go, without at least some kind of explanation, I mean, it would hardly make sense, would it? His job here can't be finished.'

Kate felt a shiver run down her spine. No, it didn't make sense, unless this was his way of letting her known that he regretted what had happened. She brushed a strand of hair from her face, angry at having allowed herself to betray her feelings, despite the fact that it was he who had provoked that response.

But hadn't she also invited, even welcomed it?

'Are you all right?'

She looked up to catch Maggie's earnest expression. 'What? Oh, yes, I'm fine. Still a bit of reaction from our little drama the other day, I expect.'

Maggie laughed. 'I've been hearing all about it, at length, and you'll be pleased to hear that when I checked earlier mother and baby were doing fine. No after-effects from the anaesthetic, and baby is taking a full breast feed.'

'Well, that's good news. I'll stop by for a chat when I do my round, and check them both over. What else do we have? Any problems you particularly want me to take a look at?'

Maggie's face clouded briefly. 'Have you seen your dad yet today?'

'No. I was going to go there now, before we start the clinic. Why?' Something in the other girl's tone made her look up, her heart suddenly missing a beat. 'He's not worse?'

'No, at least . . . well, he had another rigor. He's all right, honestly. It didn't last too long, about an hour. His temperature went up to forty-one degrees and he complained of a headache, but then the symptoms began to subside. It wasn't a full-blown attack.' She stressed the words. 'I've checked his temperature this morning, and it's almost back to normal.'

Kate listened in stunned, angry silence. 'But why wasn't I told? I deliberately didn't go in to see him last night because it was late and he was sleeping.'

Maggie interrupted her. 'Dr Ramsey didn't want you to be worried, when, as he said, the attack turned out to be a minor one and passed quickly anyway.'

'You mean, he was actually here at the time?' Kate asked indignantly.

'Yes, and thank heavens he was. In fact, it's probably thanks to the fact that he was able to administer medication straight away that helped to prevent the attack being any worse than it was.' Maggie closed the filing cabinet drawer. 'It was jolly lucky that Dr Ramsey had taken to calling in and spending some time chatting to your dad.'

Kate felt dazed. 'Yes, it was. But it doesn't alter the fact that I don't think he had any right to keep from me the fact that Dad had an attack!'

'I'm sure he was only trying to save you from worrying unnecessarily.' Maggie's voice was conciliatory. 'Besides, you said yourself, it was late by the time you got back, and your dad was sleeping comfortably. What could you have done?'

'I don't know. Probably nothing,' Kate said grudgingly. 'I just wish I'd known, that's all.'

'If there had been any question of your father being in any danger, Dr Ramsey would have seen to it that you were informed immediately. As it was, he had the situation under control with the minimum of fuss, and he was right when he said that by this morning your dad would be feeling much brighter. Besides,' she cast a shrewd look in Kate's direction, 'he said you deserved your day off. He was thinking of you.'

If only she could believe that, thought Kate with a pang, but she had fallen into the trap once too often, of thinking she knew what was going on in Jake Ramsey's mind, only to be proved wrong yet again.

She gave a rueful smile. 'I'm sorry; you're right. It would probably only have made things worse and added to Dad's worries if I'd turned up.' She closed the report book. 'We'd better make a start on the clinic. We've got a lot to get through.' Her actions were purely mechanical. She was still trying to come to terms with the fact that Jake had gone, that he wasn't going to come striding through the door, and a feeling of hurt washed over her.

To outward appearances at least, however, it was just another day. Her personal feelings had to be pushed aside as professionalism took over. It wasn't going to be so easy to shut out her feelings in private, but, at least, for the next few hours she would be kept fully occupied and have no time to think of anything but the job in hand.

Watched by a group of naked and totally uninhibited children, Kate sat perched on the edge of her seat, listening to the gentle bubbling and whistling of an elderly patient's congested lungs. The man spoke no English, so Nori interpreted, explaining gently that the medicine she was prescribing would drive the evil *mana* away.

'Tell him it will bring good *mana*, and he will soon be well again. But he must take all the medicine.' She laid heavy emphasis on the latter.

Nori translated her words, holding the man's gnarled hand, touching him as he spoke, before straightening up. 'He says the *vele* man has put a curse on him, so that your medicine will make no difference. The *vele* has stronger magic.'

Kate fought a feeling of anger. She knew how strong the belief in ancient spirits of good and evil was, especially among the older people on the islands. Her only defence against superstition was to try and fight such ignorance, without appearing to offer any direct challenge. Even so, her cheeks were flushed as she met Nori's gaze.

'This man has chronic bronchitis, which is going to get a lot worse unless he can be persuaded to take the medication.'

'I know that,' Nori said. 'I've explained that your medicine is as powerful as that of the *vele*, but he is afraid of upsetting the spirits.'

Kate bit her lip. 'Those spirits will kill him unless we can make him see sense.'

'Let me try again.' Nori took the tablets from her outstretched hand, and once again dropped to his knee to speak to the man. Kate watched, fascinated, seeing the easily recognisable expression of fear on his face, until he stretched out his hand and Nori let the tablets run into his palm.

'What did you say to him?'

'I told him that if his *mana* was so strong, he had nothing to fear from your magic. if his *mana* was displeased, it would win. If not, he would get well. He says he will put it to the test.'

Kate's eyes flashed her gratitude. 'The only thing that matters is that he gets better.'

Maggie caught her eye. 'Can you take a look at this?' She stood back as Kate lifted a man's shirt to study a curious lesion on his skin. 'I thought at first it was an infected bite. Now I'm not so sure.'

'Mm, I see what you mean.' Kate gazed thoughtfully at the sore. 'You could be right. It is a bite, of a kind.' Gently she probed the surrounding area, which was red and inflamed. 'It looks to me like cutaneous leishmaniasis. It's transmitted by the bite of sandflies. There are variations of the disease. Luckily we can treat it quite straightforwardly with an antimony-based drug.'

Having scrubbed her hands, Kate turned to her next patient, smiling reassuringly as the woman who lowered herself into the seat. There was no attempt at an answering smile. The woman, who might have been anything between thirty and fifty years old, was painfully thin and she sat listlessly, her eyes half-closed, one had lifted occasionally to brush wearily over her eyes.

Kate's face registered nothing of what was going through her mind as she spoke to the woman, persuading her to lie on a mat beneath an open canopy as she made a thorough examination. Even the slightest pressure on the woman's abdomen drew response, showing that she was in severe pain. Turning to Maggie, Kate said softly, 'You may have seen more cases like this than I have. Tell me what you think.'

Maggie questioned the woman, listening carefully to her stumbling replies before looking at Kate. 'Well, the obvious abdominal pain, combined with the general debility and inertia, make it seem like a pretty obvious case of hookworm. It's not particularly prevalent here, but

I've seen several cases.'

Kate nodded. 'It's fairly crippling, unless it's treated. The parasite gets into the skin, travels to the lungs in the bloodstream and from there, via the windpipe and gullet, to the intestine. Again, luckily, we can treat it. Let's try medication. With a bit of luck, we should get good results in a fairly short time. Unfortunately it takes longer to change standards of personal hygiene and sanitation. We can clear this infestation now, but I'll lay odds it will recur.'

Maggie, dispensing the medication, was more philosophical, 'You can't win them all. You can only do your best.'

Even if, at times, it does seem grossly inadequate, thought Kate.

The afternoon was spent sitting at her desk, trying to instil some sort of order into the remaining paperwork and to compile a list of supplies which would be needed, regardless of who sat in the chair when she was gone. She spent an hour sitting with her father. He seemed tired and reluctant to talk, and she came away feeling that, without knowing how, she was in some way letting him down. Why was it that he could talk so easily with Jake, and yet whenever she came near it was as if a barrier came down, shutting her out? Yet, strangely enough, far from resenting the fact, she found herself wishing that Jake were here now, and that he would come walking through the door.

She came back to reality with a start as Maggie came into the office, flicking on a light. 'Taken to sitting in the dark? Or do the figures look better that way?'

Kate gazed ruefully down at the papers on the desk, firmly pushing them away. 'They don't seem to improve whichever way I look at them. Anyway, that will soon be someone else's problem.' She got to her feet, conscious, as always, of the rivulets of sweat sticking the thin cotton dress to her body. 'I was just going off-duty. I've been promising myself a drink and shower, not necessarily in that order. Did you want to see me for anything specific?'

'Not really. I'm off myself any time now, but I thought you'd like to know that our diabetic patient with the head injuries is stabilising nicely. His name is David Vouza, by the way. Apparently he was fishing at the time of the accident. He lost consciousness because of the low sugar, and gave his head a nasty crack on the side of the canoe as he went into the water.'

'He was pretty lucky there was someone around to pull him out.'

'That's what I told him, but I get the feeling he's not impressed.' Maggie chuckled. 'I've heard some pretty strong language on some of the sheep stations back home, but this one beats the lot. I've tried explaining that he's going to need regular medication but I reckon this one will go walkabout rather than let anyone near him with a needle.'

'Oh, dear. Perhaps I'd better try and get through to him.'

Maggie grinned. 'I hate to risk denting your confidence, but the staff are already running a book on your chances. At the moment it's ten to one.'

'You mean ten to one I win?'

Maggie's grin widened. 'You lose. Right now he's sleeping.'

'In that case, I'll leave him to it. I'm more than happy to live to fight another day. Right now, I'm going home to put my feet up.'

'Sounds like a good idea.'

Kate looked at her. 'Why not come over? Unless you've something else to do?'

'No, as a matter of fact, I haven't, and I'd love to. I'll hand over here, get showered and changed and see you later.'

Maggie looked appreciatively round the tastefully furnished sitting-room, with its rattan chairs and table, the chintz cushions, well-stocked bookshelves and the lamps which gave out a gentle glow. 'I love this room.'

Kate smiled as she placed a tray of coffee on the low table. 'So do I. It came as something of a pleasant surprise when I first arrived. I think I'd expected something a little more ...'

'Primitive?' Maggie leaned back in her chair, visibly unwinding. 'I know what you mean.

Actually, your father brought most of this stuff with him. Don't ask me how. It just seemed to arrive, piece by piece, balanced on a canoe. Bits of England arriving by sea.'

Kate laughed. 'That sounds about right.' Her gaze softened. 'Dad has a lot of memories invested in some of these things. Books, pictures, personal things.' She broke off to pour coffee. 'Sorry about the powdered milk. I'll never get used to it. Do you want to sit here or on the veranda?'

'Here will do nicely.' Maggie accepted her cup and settled back comfortably. 'I don't think I could move even if I wanted to.'

'I know what you mean. Back at St James's, where I did my training, I'd come off-duty after a long stint and literally collapse on to a bed and sleep for twelve hours. That was a time when life seemed to consist of nothing but work and sleep.' She pulled a face. 'I'm beginning to notice distinct similarities.'

'You must have felt it was worth it.'

'Once I had that piece of paper saying I'd qualified, yes, it was worth every minute, every sleepless night.'

'It must have come as quite a shock, having to leave in your post-grad year to come out here.'

'I suppose it was,' Kate murmured hesitantly. 'Except that at the time I hadn't made any specific plans. I would have had to finish my post-grad year anyway, and I was too worried about Dad to think beyond that.'

'So, what will you do when you get back home?'

'I don't know,' Kate said wearily. 'It's something I've put off thinking about. I'll probably go into general practice somewhere or I may go back to St James's , if there's a place for me. I've even been toying with the idea of doing obstetrics. It's not something I'd considered before, but, well, now I quite like the idea.'

'This wouldn't have anything to do with our most recent arrival?'

'It could,' Kate admitted wryly. 'If nothing else, it made me aware of my own inadequacies. How about you?'

'Me?' Maggie gazed down at her cup. 'Actually, I've been thinking it might be a good time to go back home, to Sydney.'

'But why?' Kate couldn't hide her astonishment. 'I thought you loved it out here.'

'Yes, I do. But that has a lot to do with the people I've worked with, as much as the place itself. Besides, I've done two years. More than I'd originally planned.'

Kate teased lightly, 'You realise that this would be a lot of people's idea of paradise?'

'Maybe that's part of the trouble. Sometimes it doesn't seem real. On the surface at least, it's almost too perfect.' Maggie drained the last of her coffee, and put the cup down. 'I think it's time I went and took another look at the real world, the one I used to belong to. It would be too easy to stay here and let everything else drift by. Do you understand what I mean?'

'I think I do,' Kate replied shakily. 'But have you made any plans?'

'Nothing definite. I reckon I'd get a job in Sydney easily enough. Or I might apply to one of the other health organisations. I was talking to Jake . . . I mean, Dr Ramsey.'

'I thought you didn't go in for formality out here.'

'No, well, I was talking to him about it, about the possibility of being sent somewhere else. Africa, maybe. It's something I've been thinking about for some time, and he seemed to think I'd have no trouble getting a posting. As a matter of fact, I got the impression he was thinking of moving on himself in the not too distant future.'

Kate flinched. 'You mean, he's thinking of leaving the organisation? To do what? Go where?'

Maggie yawned. 'He didn't say specifically. I may even have misunderstood.'

Kate felt a sudden tightness around her heart. What . . . what about his family? Don't they care that he spends his life flying from one side of the world to the other?'

Maggie didn't look up. 'I imagine his wife must be used to it by now.'

With a supreme effort of will Kate managed to meet Maggie's gaze. 'Jake . . . is married?' She was

surprised to hear her voice sounding strangely
normal when every nerve in her body suddenly
seemed to be screaming. 'Did he tell you that?'

Maggie was stifling another yawn. 'Not in so
many words. Just something about a girl he was
in medical school with. Though, come to think of
it, I suppose he must have done. He mentioned
the fact that she was a doctor, too.' Maggie
regarded her intently. 'I thought you knew.'

Kate tried to focus her gaze through a blur of
faintness. 'No. He's never talked about his family.
I just assumed . . .' The words came thinly out of
the tight constriction of her throat. She felt as if
she had suddenly experienced a devastating loss.
Yet how could she lose what she had never had?

Jake was married. It explained so much—but
the kind of restless energy that seemed to repent
any attempt to tie him down. And not why he'd
kissed her. That was what seemed so unfair. She
had been purely physical, nothing more. He had
found her sexually attractive and she had read too
much into it.

Only now did it occur to her that they hadn't
even said goodbye. Or had they, and she just
hadn't realised it? Looking back, there had been
something so final about the way he had walked
away.

If only she had known. But, even if she had,
what could she had done to change things?

CHAPTER EIGHT

THE following two days were almost an anticlimax, thought Kate. As if she were waiting for something to happen, without exactly knowing what. All of which contrived to add to her depression, and made her resolve to throw herself into her work, grateful to find that exhaustion drove most things out of her mind, at least for a while.

The morning clinic over, she went along to her father's room and found him out of bed, sitting by the window. He was still very pale and, suddenly, his weight loss seemed more apparent. But Kate was shaken to see that he was dressed, his dressing-gown lying discarded on the bed.

For a moment, as she went towards him, her heart pounded, but his eyes flickered open as she stood uncertainty.

'Kate, my dear.'

'Dad, what are you doing out of bed, and why are you dressed?' She bent to kiss his cheek.

'Because I hate lying in bed, I'm not used to it, and don't intend to start now.' John Tyson closed the book which lay open on his lap, gesturing her affably to a chair. 'I hope you're not intending to deliver a lecture.'

She smiled. 'You deserve it.'

'I'm too old to start taking orders.'

'Nonsense, you're forty-nine.'

'Fifty.'

She let it pass. 'What's this?' She pointedly eyed a pile of papers on the bedside table. 'You've been working!'

'A few things I should have cleared up ages ago, but never got around to, Letters, that's all.'

Kate looked at him reproachfully. 'You aren't supposed to over-exert yourself.'

'Rubbish. A little exercise is good for me.'

'Little being the operative word.'

He had the grace to look sheepish, 'I didn't realise I'd raised a daughter who was a bully.'

'Well, now you know,' She laughed. 'Anyway, why do you have to worry about this kind of thing now?'

'Because I've been putting things off for far too long. It's too easy to dismiss things as being unimportant. Besides, I don't like loose ends. Never did. Can't abide them.'

'Oh, Dad.' Kate bit her lip.

'Now, now. I'm being sensible. Things have to be done. I've no regrets.'

'How can you say that, when you've done so much—'

'It's time someone else had a chance.' He took her hand in his. 'I've made up my mind and, besides, I'm tired.' He laughed wryly. 'On a practical level, I'm also too old. Yes,' he said as she shook her head. 'It needs someone younger, someone with fresh energy and ideas and commitment to carry on here.'

'But you have commitment.'

'Had,' he said softly. 'But it wasn't purely one-sided. I gained a lot from being here, too. It saved my sanity after your mother died.' he broke off. 'You see, my reasons for staying were purely selfish.'

'No.' Kate blinked hard on the tears that stung behind her lashes. 'I don't believe that.'

'Well, be that as it may, I won't be sorry to be going home. Any more than I shall be sorry right now to get out of here.'

Kate stared at him. 'What do you mean? Get out of here?'

'Precisely that.' John Tyson gave her a no-nonsense look as he rose slowly to his feet. 'My bag is packed. I'm moving back to the bungalow.'

'Dad, do you really think that's wise?'

'Infinitely,' he stated. 'In the first place it will make far less work for the staff if I scatter my papers elsewhere.'

Kate fixed him with a meaningful stare. 'I'm being serious.'

'I can see you are.' He eyed her wryly. 'But age still has certain advantages, stubbornness being one of them. My mind is made up.'

'But you still need rest and regular medication.'

'I have a bed, and I think I can still be relied

upon to measure the correct dosage from a bottle.'

'Oh, Dad.' She gritted her teeth then forced herself to relax. 'You've been very ill. The rigors can happen at any time, and there's no way of knowing how severe they may be.' She broke off with a sigh of exasperation as he packed his book into an open bag which stood on a chair. 'Look, why am I telling you all this? You're a doctor. You know the consequences.'

'Then let me be the judge of what's best,' he said gravely. 'I know what I'm doing, Kate. I'm still in full command of my faculties.'

She looked away, blinking hard. 'You always were as stubborn as a mule.'

'I suspect it's a family trait.' A large, firm hand closed over hers. 'I don't need constant nursing care. Besides, Jake has done all the tests he needs to do and he agrees.'

She stared at him, disbelief and confusion vying for a place. 'He . . . he does?'

'We've had quite a few long chats. It was nice being able to discuss old times, catch up on all the news.'

Kate had the distinct feeling that she was deliberately being side tracked. 'Yes, I'm sure it was. But these tests—'

'Oh, all pretty much routine stuff. Nothing to worry about.' John Tyson's hand rose in a dismissive gesture. 'I could have told him the results myself. I shall get a great deal of pleasure out of doing just that when he gets back.'

He wasn't looking at her, which was just as well or he might have seen the tide of colour which washed up in Kate's cheeks.

'He's coming back to the island? He hasn't left for good?'

John Tyson looked at her rather oddly. 'What made you think that?'

'Oh, I . . . nothing. I just thought . . .' Her voice sounded a like a hoarse whisper. 'He didn't say goodbye.'

'Perhaps he's not the kind of man who likes goodbyes. Some don't.' His gaze swept her face. 'Or perhaps he didn't know anyone cared.'

Kate couldn't look at him, she was too afraid of what her face might show. She took refuge in severity. 'I'm still not happy about you leaving here and going back to the bungalow. You know I can't be there as much as I'd like.'

'Well, you'll have to take that up with Jake.' He smiled good-naturedly. 'In the meantime, I've asked Benjamin to collect my bags. He should be here any minute now.' He placed a hand over hers. 'I know what I'm doing, and I accept responsibility for my actions.'

Kate knew the words were meant to reassure, but somehow she couldn't imagine Jake would see it that way.

It was late afternoon by the time she had caught

up with the clinic session and finally managed to finish a ward round. She was seeing the last patient with Sue Ling when Maggie came towards them, her face troubled.

'You'd better come quickly. We've got a problem. A child has been badly injured. He was fishing with some older boys in the lagoon, and fell out of the canoe. A shark must have got past the reef.'

'Oh, God, no!' Kate was already on her feet, handing over to Sue Ling and heading for the door. 'How bad is it?'

Maggie shook her head. Her face was white. 'Strewth, I've seen some pretty nasty sights, but this . . . It must have gone for the boy's leg. It could have been worse, but not much.'

Kate was running beside her. 'But sharks don't usually attack unless they scent blood.'

'I know, I gather the boy had cut his finger on a fish hook before he went into the water.'

Kate pushed open the door that led to the small emergency treatment-room. At a glance her eyes took in the child, seemingly covered in blood, as he lay on the examination couch. Nori was helping to comfort a distraught women. Several others milled around as two nursing assistants did their best to stem the tide of blood which was pouring from a hideous wound.

Kate moved in, feeling her stomach tighten. 'Who are all these people?' she demanded.

Nori glanced up. 'This is the boy's mother. The

rest are relatives.'

'Well, if they want the child to stand any chance at all, they must get of here *now*, and let us do what has to be done. We need room to work.' Her voice softened. 'Please, Nori, explain to them. We have to move fast if we're going to stop the bleeding and try to reduce the shock.' She was shrugging herself into a gown held by one of the assistants, vaguely aware that Nori had turned and was speaking to the anxious crowd, but she was too intent on assessing the extent of the wound to notice that the room somehow, magically, cleared.

'Get a drip set up, and treat the shock first.' Kate muttered through gritted teeth as she swiftly administered a pain-killing injection. The child had, mercifully, drifted into unconsciousness. 'Let's get antibiotic powder over this area here.' She moved aside as Maggie's gloved hand applied a liberal dusting. 'These splinters of bone will have to come out.'

Kate wiped the back of her hand across her forehead before bending once again over the child. 'It's not quite as bad as I expected, though that's not saying much. I'm amazed he survived at all. Sharks don't usually miss.'

'I gather his friends were beating the water with paddles while they dragged him out.'

Kate nodded. 'He's lost a lot of blood. I'll need some thin silk and extra-fine sutures. How's his blood pressure?'

'Falling.'

'I'm not surprised. He's in deep shock. Give me suction here, I can't see what I'm doing. Benjamin, we shall need plaster once I've reset his foot.' She wished Jake were there. He would know what to do. But he wasn't, and she had no right to wish it. So she must do the best she could.

Easing her back, she bent again to complete a row of sutures, frowning as she finally straightened up. 'He's lucky. The shark obviously didn't have a chance to get hold or there wouldn't have been anything left to patch up. He'll have scars, but at least he'll live.'

It was another hour before the patient was wheeled out of the small operating theatre and Kate was able to drag off her gown and mask. Nori was waiting for her as she walked into the small office.

'He'll be fine.' She gave the quick assurance, and heard his sharp intake of breath. 'He should be left to sleep, but his parents can take a quick look at him as long as they leave again almost immediately. I shall have to warn his mother about the scars.'

'His mother will live with that. Better than to lose her son the same way she lost her husband.'

Kate stared at him, feeling the colour drain from her face. She told herself it was tiredness and reaction setting in. 'I can see why she was so concerned for her son.'

'You're tired. When does Dr Ramsey return?'

'I don't know. Soon, I imagine.'

Nori's eyes darkened. 'Then you will be leaving the islands?'

Kate swallowed painfully. 'Perhaps, after all, it's for the best. Dad needs me, Nori. Oh, he won't admit it, but . . . we haven't spent a great deal of time together these past few years and, now, I feel it's important that we should.' She shook her head. 'I can't explain it.'

Nori reached out to take her hands in his. 'The islanders have a saying. The translation is not precise, but we say that love strides oceans, making a bridge to bring back those we hold dear.'

Kate's eyes filled with tears. 'I hope it's true, Nori. I do hope so.'

His eyes swept her face. 'Your man will return.' He looked at her for a moment longer, then let her go. 'Our people never say goodbye. They believe that as long as the many memory lives, so too does the friendship, no matter how many miles separate us from those we love.'

Kate would have given anything to believe the simple philosophy. But wasn't it just that, too simple? Too naïve? And anyway, Jake wasn't her man. True, he was coming back, but she was the only one doing the loving, and it seemed the path was only one way!

'I'll walk you back to the bungalow.'

'There's no need.' She smiled.

'No need, but I like to walk with you.'

Kate looked at Nori, then put her hand in his. After all, how many more times would there be?

The sun had gone down, and Kate shivered slightly as they walked along the shore towards the bungalow.

'You're cold,' Nori said.

'No, I don't know what it was. A ghost walking over my grave.' The faint breeze coming off the sea stirred the palms, and in the darkness she could just make out the twinkling lanterns from the canoes, bobbing out in the lagoon.

Slipping off her shoes, Kate let the warm sand trickle between her toes and suddenly, in spite of her tiredness, she felt reluctant to move. There was something so infinitely soothing about the sound of water sighing against the sand.

As they reached the bungalow, she turned to Nori. 'I'll see you in the morning. Goodnight, Nori.'

'Come to the beach later and swim. All the young people will be there.'

At any other time she would have been tempted, but not tonight. For some reason she just wanted to be alone. 'It's been a long day and I'm tired.'

'Then I'll dance for you.' Pulling her gently towards him, Nori kissed her before turning to disappear into the darkness.

Kate wearily climbed the steps and let herself

into the bungalow, but she stopped as the door swung to a close behind her. Her mouth felt suddenly very dry. Something was wrong. The room was in darkness. But why? Lighting the lamps was something Selena always did.

A tiny bubble of panic welled up and then, before she could move, light flared, suffusing the room with a pale glow. In the few seconds it took her eyes to adjust she saw the figure move and come towards her.

CHAPTER NINE

KATE felt as if her legs had turned to jelly as he moved out of the shadows, then she heard herself gasp as the all too familiar features took shape in the halo of light from the lamp.

'Jake!' she exclaimed. Panic gave way to relief and some other emotion she had to resist putting a name to. 'But how . . .?'

'Just what the hell do you think you're doing?' he demanded.

Shock held her rigid as she stared at him. Her moment of happiness died, swept away by the expression of anger on his face. 'Wh . . . what do you mean?'

Jake's tone was sardonic. 'I mean you owe me an explanation, Doctor, and it had better be good.'

Kate met his startling blue eyes. 'If I had any idea what you were talking about——'

'Oh, for God's sake, spare me the look of outraged innocence!' He drew a hand wearily across his forehead, then his face tightened. 'You know very well what I'm talking about. I want to know on whose authority you discharged your father from the hospital, where he was being treated as my patient? Didn't they teach you anything about ethics in medical school?'

Kate knew he cheeks were scarlet with angry colour as she faced him. 'Now wait a minute——' She broke off, her gaze going to the door of her father's room.

'He's sleeping. I checked.'

She glared at him, but lowered her voice. 'Now wait a minute. What do you mean, why *I* discharged him? You don't seriously imagine that *I* approved of Dad leaving the hospital? I understood that *you* had agreed.'

'Is that likely?' Jake demanded drily.

'But . . . I understood that you carried out all the tests.'

Jake's look was sharp. 'Yes, it's true, I have. At least those I was able to do with the limited equipment you have available here.'

'I see.' Kate swallowed hard, wondering why her feeling of anger should fade, only to be replaced by a growing sense of alarm. 'Actually,' she gave a shaky laugh as her gaze flew up to meet his. 'I don't understand at all.'

He studied her for a moment. 'How about a drink? I could certainly do with one, and you look as if you need it.'

'I'll make some coffee.' She was heading for the kitchen when Jake's voice stopped her.

'Not coffee. Brandy,' he said.

She turned slowly to face him, fear becoming almost tangible, something to be held off as long as she didn't give a name to it.

'Shall I get it? he said quietly.

kate was surprised to find that she was shaking as she watched him pour the amber liquid, handing a glass to her. She took a sip, feeling its warmth steal down her throat, but it didn't seem to stop her shaking.

'Drink it all.'

She shook her head. ' I think I need to stay sober, Jake.'

He moved closer, lifting her face so that she was forced to look at him. Holding her by the shoulders, he drew her close, then, with a long, shuddering sigh, he bent his head and kissed her. His lips moved on hers, feeling the tremor of a response she was too weak to deny. Nothing seemed to matter but the seeking urgency of his mouth on hers. Kate clung to him, forgetting everything but the sheer ecstasy of being in his arms. It was several seconds before he released her. 'Trust me,' he whispered raggedly.

'I do.' Her throat tightened uncontrollably. 'But you're going to have to explain, Jake. I need to understand what's happening.'

He drew her closer into his arms. 'Kate, your father is a very sick man.'

She didn't move; somehow she needed the reassuring sound of his heartbeat. 'That's why you were doing tests.'

'Yes,' he murmured thickly. 'And it's the reason I went away for a few days. Because I needed to verify some of the results and bring back supplies of a particular drug.'

This time he felt her tense, then her head jerked back. Are you saying that he's worse?' She stared at him. 'I know the repeated bouts of malaria, and then the pneumonia . . .'

His hands tightened on her arms. 'Kate, it isn't the malaria, though it must have contributed. God knows, I only wish it were.' His blue eyes appealed to her silently. Kate knew she should say something, but somehow the words wouldn't come. 'Kate, your father has a heart condition. If he isn't operated on within the next few months, he will die.'

She became aware of him looking at her sharply, and saw the lines of tiredness etched into his own face. She felt herself sway, heard his voice, coming as if from a long way away, at the end of a long, dark tunnel, then the room was spinning and she was falling, drifting into the blackness which reached up to take her in its grasp.

It was Jake's voice that brought her back to reality. Then, as she forced her eyes to open, a blurred face swam into view, bending lower, so close that it was almost touching hers. 'You're all right, my love. You fainted, that's all.'

At least, she thought that he had called her 'my love' before strong arms had gathered her up and had deposited her gently, but firmly, on the couch. Dimly she registered that he had left her, but within seconds he had returned and was pressing a glass into her hands. 'Here, drink this.' She tried to push the glass away, but he insisted, 'It's only water this time, with a couple of tablets. They'll help you to feel better.'

She felt herself supported gently, too miserable to argue as memory returned. She swallowed the tablets, then sat up. 'I'm all right now. Sorry, it was a ridiculous thing to do.'

'Perfectly understandable under the circumstances. I wish I could have found some better way to break the news.'

'It wasn't your fault. It ... it just came as a shock. In fact, I'm not still sure I've taken it in properly. You said Dad has a heart condition,' she said wearily. 'How could I have missed a thing like that?'

'Quite easily, especially as he made pretty sure you wouldn't suspect. I almost missed it myself, until I talked to you and realised we were both coming up against the same blank wall.'

Kate moistened her dry lips with her tongue. 'You're saying that he knew, and deliberately kept it from us?'

Jake's mouth twisted. 'It was pretty easy. We were fooled by the symptoms of the malaria and then the pneumonia, except that we both started asking the same questions. Why was he still so weak and not making any apparent progress?'

'But why?' Kate stared at him.

'Because he's a stubborn man. Because he didn't want you to worry, and probably because he was trying to convince himself that it wasn't serious. I noticed the breathlessness for myself when I talked to him,' Jake said quietly.' He admitted, after some probing that he's been getting chest pain.'

Bereft of words, Kate shook her head.

'His whole history is against him,' Jake said grimly. 'Repeated bouts of malaria, blackwater fever. He's anaemic, and then he admitted his childhood history.'

Kate stared up at him. 'What do you mean?'

'Kate, he had rheumatic fever at the age of fifteen. Not a severe bout, but enough. It must have caused damage he knew nothing about until now.' He felt her shudder.

'You're saying . . . he's in danger of having a coronary.'

'What I'm saying is that he needs urgent medical investigation with a view to possible corrective surgery. There could be valve damage.' His mouth tightened. 'Damn it, I wish I could do more myself, but he needs the sort of care and facilities we don't possess here. He has to be got back to England. Even that has its risks. He needs absolute rest, no exertion.'

Kate closed her eyes briefly. 'And if they operate? What chance does he have?'

'Don't ask me to make judgements like that, my darling.'

Kate knew the colour had drained from her face. Her medical training, her whole experience of dealing with sick people had somehow failed to prepare her for this. She didn't know how to cope. When someone she loved desperately needed her most, she was going to pieces.

'If he dies I'll never forgive myself.'

'Don't say that.' Jake's hand tightened on her arm. 'This isn't your fault. There was nothing, *nothing* you could have done to prevent it.'

'But I should have realised.'

'How could you?' He drew her closer, wrapping his arms around her. 'He made sure you wouldn't. I would have been fooled, too, if he hadn't realised for himself that time was running out.' He put her from him just far enough to brush the tears from her cheeks. 'He has to go home, Kate, and he'll need you with him.'

She nodded, her jaw too tight with tension for speech for several seconds. 'How . . . soon?'

'I've already made the arrangements for you both to fly out in a few days' time. It'll mean you have to go over to the big island first, but we can fix that. I managed to put a number of phone calls through to England. It took a while, but I finally got to speak to someone I know at St James's. It's all settled. You'll be met by ambulance at the airport, and your father will be admitted straight away.'

Kate listened, feeling a chill beginning to gather

round her heart. She lifted her head to look at him.
'Will you operate?'

Jake shook his head. 'I'm not a cardiologist and
your father needs specialist techniques, but I've
spoken to Steve Collins, a colleague of mine.'

Kate blinked her tears determinedly away. 'I
think I remember him.'

'He's the best there is. You can have absolute
faith in him.'

She forced a smile to her lips. His nearness was
almost unbearable, the longing to stay in his arms
like a physical pain. 'What about you? Will you be
coming back to England?'

It was as if a shutter came down over his
expression. 'I can't. Not immediately. There are
things I still have to do before I can make specific
plans.'

There was a real tightness in her throat as she
looked at him. Why was she tormenting herself
like this? Asking questions she had no right to ask?
'I heard you might be offered a new job.'

'It's a possibility,' he said abruptly. 'But at the
moment that's all it is, and until things are more
certain I prefer not to discuss it. I *can't* discuss
it.'

She drew herself up, the muscles of her face
tense lest she betray her feelings for him. 'I see.'

'Are you all right?'

She looked up to see him frowning. 'Yes, I'm
fine. I won't faint again, if that's what's worrying

you.'

'It wasn't,' he said tautly. 'You'll need time to pack if you're leaving in five days' time.'

'Five days!'

'There's no time to lose. The sooner your father begins his treatment the better. Nothing else matters.'

He was right, of course, but her head was suddenly reeling at the speed with which everything seemed to be happening.

'There's a plane out on Friday. You'll need to cross to the big island at least twenty-four hours before.'

It was sensible, logical, and it was tearing her apart.

His hands came down on her shoulders and her heart missed a beat. He cupped her face in his hands and looked at her for a long, tense moment. 'Kate . . .'

Her breath seemed to catch in her throat. 'Yes?'

His hands tightened until they were in danger of bruising her flesh, then abruptly he released her. 'He has a good chance. Don't give up hope. He'll be in the best possible hands.'

Numbly Kate stared at him. Why did she get the distinct feeling that he had been about to say something quite different? That a golden moment had slipped by?

Somehow she managed to keep her features in an impassive mask as she stepped away. 'I'll have a lot to do in the next few days. I think, if you don't mind, I'll get an early night.'

After he had gone, she lay for a long time staring into the darkness. What could he have said? What could either of them have said that would have made any difference? Jake had a wife. She was going back to England. There was no point in fooling herself that her feelings for Jake would ever change. The most she could hope for was that, by making a new life, she would somehow learn to live without him.

CHAPTER TEN

KATE stared disconsolately at the rain as it lashed against the windows of the medical staff lounge. In the three weeks since she had arrived back in England, it seemed to have done nothing but rain. Or perhaps there had been fine days and she simply hadn't noticed.

There was an odd unreality about everything that wasn't only to do with worry over her father's health, but also to do with Jake. Every time she walked along a corridor and saw a figure coming towards her, she imagined it might be him. Her heart would start thudding each time a door opened and a white-coated figure appeared.

Those first few weeks, back at work in a busy hospital, had been exhausting, but that was the way she preferred it. It left little time for thinking, and she would be eternally grateful to Sam Redfern, the senior consultant in general surgery, who had been more than ready to answer her plea for work.

Sam was a Yorkshire man. Stout and fatherly. He also knew John Tyson, and had been struck by the incredible likeness between father and daughter from the moment Kate had walked into his office.

'You'll want to be close, that's natural.'

'I also need to be kept busy, Sam. The last thing I need is time to think.'

He had looked at her across the desk. 'I was going to suggest it anyway.'

'I don't want any favours.'

He gave a loud bellow of a laugh. 'And I won't be doing you any! How do you fancy a spell on Accident and Emergency? As it happens, we're having trouble finding a replacement for the chap who left about a month back. Took himself off to foreign parts. Of course, it may not be what you had in mind. A and E's not everyone's cup of tea. And it would be on a temporary basis, mind.'

'No, no. I'll take it. It suits me just fine. I don't feel I can plan too far ahead, not yet anyway.'

'Aye, well, that's natural enough, but we'll look on your temporary need as our gain.'

On the surface, at least, she was cool and in control, brushing aside concerned queries about her own health with what was becoming a practised ease. She knew she looked tired. Dark smudges beneath her eyes were evidence of near-sleepless nights. She had lost weight, too. 'Change of air, change of diet,' she would say. It was easy enough to come up with excuses that sounded perfectly logical. Everyone knew she was worried about her father. Broken hearts were easy to hide.

She poured herself another cup of coffee, trying

desperately not to look at the clock. Surely it couldn't take this long to carry out an examination? What were they doing? What was Jake doing?

'Is there any coffee left?'

Kate spun round quickly, her heart racing as the male voice came from behind her. 'Mark, I didn't hear you.'

Tall and slim, the young registrar smiled. 'I'm not surprised. You were miles away.'

'Is . . . is there any news?'

'No, but it is a bit soon,' he said quickly, seeing the anxious look in her eyes. He glanced at his watch. 'It's not really all that long, you know, and Collins is thorough. he won't keep you waiting unnecessarily.' He spooned sugar into his coffee. 'How's it going, down in A and E?'

'Pretty much as I always remember it. Hectic, noisy, too many people to fill too few spaces.'

'Mm, I know what you mean.' He regarded her thoughtfully. 'I'm sure if you wanted it, there would be a place for you as a junior physician on one of the teams, you know. And it wouldn't be a favour.'

'You've been talking to Sam.'

He grinned, slightly shamefaced. 'Only in the respect that he made it clear he'd like to see you back on a permanent basis.'

Kate frowned. 'I'm not Dad, Mark.'

'I was never in any danger of thinking you were.' He gazed appreciatively at her over his cup. 'Nor is Sam. He had a lot of time for John Tyson, but he's a tough nut and he's proud of his team. If he took you on, it would be on your own merit. It would have to be—he expects the best.'

'I'm flattered.'

'Don't be. You qualified with honours. No one was more sorry than Sam when you didn't show any interest in the junior physician's job. It would have been yours for the asking.'

'I wasn't in any position to show interest.' Kate drained her coffee.

'But you could, now that things have changed. The remainder of your post-grad year will fly by——'

'Mark,' she interrupted briskly, 'I'm not ready to make any plans.'

'Hey, I'm not pressuring. Just trying to say, in my own heavy-handed way, that we'd all be happy to have you as part of the team.'

'You're very good for my morale, you know that? Damn!' She gave a sharp exclamation. 'That's my bleep. I'm wanted in A and E.'

'Just bear in mind what I've said,' he called after her. 'And welcome home.'

She smiled without answering. What was it they said? Home is where the heart is. But her heart had been left behind on an island thousands of miles away, and all she had was an ache to fill its place.

The doors swung open beneath the pressure of

her hand. Out-patients was busy as various consultants held clinics on the same day. Kate walked through, smiling at patients who looked hopefully in her direction before losing interest as she made her way through the department, through X-ray, which was equally busy, and on to A and E.

'Cubicle three. Doctor.' Sister Fields greeted Kate's arrival with a look of relief. 'A child on his bike in collision with a car.' She swept aside the curtains. 'One arm is definitely broken. We're cleaning him up now.'

Kate was already at the examination couch making a preliminary examination of the boy, who couldn't have been more than twelve years old. Her trained eye carefully assessed his condition, taking in the pale features and the clammy feel of his skin. 'We'd better have this sleeve cut away, Sister. We'll worry about the rest of his clothes when we've checked him over. I don't want him moved more than is absolutely necessary. I think there may be a skull fracture.'

Sister Fields set to work with a pair of suture scissors. 'I'll warn Theatre.'

'Anything I can do to help?' Tony Phillips, the senior casualty officer, put his head round the curtains.

'I'd welcome another pair of hands.' Kate glanced up. 'Let's get the mobile X-ray in, Sister.'

Tony Phillips moved in and began to make

gentle movements of the small limbs. 'Mn, I thought so. The collar-bone is dislocated. We'll sort that out now, Sister.'

Kate looked up. 'What about the driver of the car?'

Sister handed a steel kidney dish to a young second-year nurse. 'He's in the next cubicle. Staff Nurse is with him. He doesn't look too bad. A bump on the head, when he swerved to avoid the child and hit a parked vehicle. But I'd say his biggest headache is likely to be from the hangover he gets when he sobers up.'

Kate caught Tony Phillip's gaze. 'Do you want me to take a look at him?'

'I think you'd better. Drunks, especially drunks who knock down innocent kids, make me see red. What about the police? I take it they've been informed?'

'Waiting to interview him,' Sister confirmed. 'Nurse, I'm expecting the child's parents to arrive. When they do, put them in my office, will you, and make sure they have some tea. It will give us a chance to get him cleaned up before they see him. But make it clear that it will only be very briefly, before he goes to Theatre.'

'Will do, Sister.'

'Who's doing the list today?'

'Baker, as far as I know,' Kate said. 'I'm glad. He's good; if anyone can sort this little chap out, he can.'

'Dr Phillips, we've got another RTA coming in.' A mauve-clad staff nurse peered round the curtains. 'Two drivers. They're being brought in now. I don't think one of them is going to make it.'

'I'll give a hand.' Kate inserted the last suture into a wound, and stood back. 'Theatre will need the X-rays as soon as possible, Sister.'

'I'll collect them and take them up myself, Doctor.'

Kate moved swiftly to the next cubicle where the accident victims were being wheeled in. Tony Phillips swore softly under his breath as he raised the blanket, bent to apply the stethoscope to the man's chest, then reached for an ophthalmoscope. After a few seconds he straightened up. 'This one's dead. Instantly, from the look of him. Let's hope the other one's in better shape.' He gave Kate a wry glance. 'I don't suppose you saw much of this sort of thing out on that tropical island of yours?'

She deliberately kept her gaze lowered as she reached for a pack of sterile burns dressings. 'You could say that. At least sharks don't know any better.' Her gaze rose and fell, leaving him totally incapable of guessing what had been going on in her head, and with the uncomfortable thought that perhaps he had missed a very relevant point.

'We've got one of the passengers, Doctor.' Kate stood aside as the patient was moved to the examination couch. She scarcely had time to take in the full extent of the injuries. Her actions were purely instinctive.

'His blood pressure is falling, Doctor.'

'You'd better get the neurological registrar down here for this one.' Tony glanced over his mask from the patient he was working on. 'I don't like the look of this head wound.'

'Sister, ask X-ray if they'd hurry the plates through.' Kate spoke without looking up. 'I need to see how many ribs are broken.'

'How many more are they bringing in, for heaven's sake?' Tony's voice was sharp. 'You'd better call for some assistance down here.'

The young staff nurse shook her head. 'As far as we know from the flying squad, there are no more.'

'Well, thank goodness for that!'

Time lost all meaning as they worked. It came as something of a surprise when Tony finally straightened up, tugged down his mask, and said. 'Well, it looks as if we can take a breather. How about coffee? Theatre can bleep if they need any extra assistance.'

The phone rang in Sister's office. Making her excuses, she hurried away. Kate followed the others out of the cubicle, welcoming the idea of coffee and a brief respite before the next onslaught.

'Oh, Dr Tyson,' Sister appeared from the office. 'Mr Redfern just rang through to ask if you'd mind calling in to see him when you can spare a minute.'

Kate felt the panic rising in her as she handed a bundle of case files to Tony. 'It must be the results of Dad's tests. Sorry. Can you cover here till I get back?'

'Happy to. Just go.'

She was hurrying away, a slender figure in an open white coat. Sam was waiting for her, a tray of coffee at the ready.

'Thought you might need this. Help yourself to biscuits. Sit down.'

She sat, waiting as he poured. 'Sam, I can't stand this. You obviously called me here to tell me about Dad. Can't we just get it over with?'

He handed her a cup. 'It's nothing to get in a panic about, love.'

Kate's hands tightened on the saucer. 'I take it you have had the results?'

'Right. Young Collins popped in to see me a while back.' Half seated on the edge of the desk, his eyes met hers. 'It's not good, but it's not all bad either.'

'Just tell me, Sam, please. You've known me long enough to know I'd rather have the truth. I may not like it, but I'll cope as soon as I know what it is I'm facing.'

He cleared his throat. 'Well, the tests really confirmed what we already suspected. His past history, along with the added complications of malaria, has left him in a pretty bad way. The latest

ECG shows a significant deterioration.'

Kate passed her tongue over her dry lips. 'Sam, you're telling me that it's quite definite that he needs surgery.'

'That's about the measure of it. Trouble is, he's in no shape. If only he hadn't been so cussed about letting on.'

Kate leaned forward. 'Are you saying there's some reason why you can't operate?'

'It's like this. Young Collins wants to go ahead as soon as possible, but you dad's still got a bit of an infection bubbling away there in his chest. We've got him on antibiotics. We're hoping we can clear it, with a bit of luck, in the next few days, to be able to go ahead. Provisionally, he's on the list for surgery in a week's time.'

'I see.' Ridiculously it was all she could think of to say. She wished Jake were there.

'I'd tell you to take some time off,' Sam said. 'But you said yourself, it's best to keep busy.'

Kate got to her feet. 'I still feel that way.'

'I imagine you'd like to go and see him. That's fine, but don't stay more than a few minutes. We want him to rest as much as possible.'

She nodded. 'I'll look in before I go off-duty.' Her gaze met his. 'How did he take the decision to operate?'

Sam's thick brows rose. 'He knew it was inevitable. Pity he waited so long. His chances would have been better.' He frowned. 'I gather he'd still be sitting on that island of his right now, if Jake Ramsey hadn't made him see sense. Heard anything from Jake, have you? Nice young fella. Good surgeon, too.'

'No, no, I haven't.' Kate was making for the door.

'Well, probably not surprising, really. He's more than likely still stuck in Switzerland. Could be snowed in, lucky beggar.'

Kate stared blankly. 'Switzerland? But why on earth should he be in Switzerland, of all places?'

'End of the earth, is it? Bit like Yorkshire?' Sam chuckled as a blush spread across her face. 'World Health thingy. Gathering of the all-powerful. Jake was giving 'em a talking to.' He glanced curiously and with some concern at her pale features. 'Thought you'd know. Been one of his pet projects for the past three years, raising funds for small mission hospitals, refugee camps and the like.' He frowned. 'Not surprising, really, what with that business with his wife and all.'

'Sam.' Kate's mouth trembled. 'I don't understand a word you're saying. What about . . . Jake's wife?'

'Married a girl he did his training with. Brilliant doctor, too, was Helen. A couple of years older than Jake.' His face clouded. 'Probably just as well there weren't any kids. It near enough finished him when she was killed.'

Kate's mouth felt dry. She had to swallow hard before she could speak. 'Jake's wife is dead?'

Sam ran a hand through the thick bush of grey hair. 'Rotten business. Seems she left the refugee camp she was working in, during one of those ceasefires, to try and get food and medical supplies. Some sniper got her on the way back.'

Kate knew the colour had drained from her face, leaving it ashen. 'Sam, I had no idea.'

'Not something he talks about.'

Jake's wife was dead. Kate turned and walked blindly from the room. What a complete and utter fool she had been. It all seemed so clear now, the reason he had shown so little eagerness to stay in one place, to go home. He must have felt he had nothing to go back to. It also explained why he had let her go so easily. He was still in love with his wife. Yet could she have been so completely mistaken when she had believed those kisses had meant something to him too?

CHAPTER ELEVEN

KATE climbed into bed feeling both physically and mentally exhausted, praying she would sleep. An hour later she was still awake, staring into he darkness. If she tried really hard, she could shut out the noise of passing traffic and pretend instead that she was listening to the sound of surf, breaking over the reef, or that she was back in the bungalow, the scent of flowers drifting in through the open window.

'And any minute now you'll be telling yourself that Jake is going to come striding in through that door. Dreams! she told herself fiercely, as she punched her pillow for the tenth time. He made it quite clear that you had no part in his life, and the sooner you learn to live with that fact, the better.

The moon disappeared behind a cloud. Perhaps it was time she made a move, too, tried to get some sort of order into her life. Somewhere there must be a small, out-of-town practice, where she could make a comfortable enough living as a junior partner. She would have to buy a small house or flat, big enough for her father to remain independent and for each of them to retain a certain amount of privacy, while at the same time she could be on hand . . .

She had fallen asleep with nothing resolved, and the thought was still with her for the next afternoon as she walked through X-ray into the department.

Tony was with a registrar. He acknowledged her arrival with a grin, but was obviously too involved to stop and talk.

Sister Fields came out of her office without her customary harassed look.

'Quiet today, aren't we Sister?'

'Just give it time. Things will start to hot up, then we'll be lucky if we get time to breathe. Would you take a look at these X-rays for me, Doctor? A young chappie was brought in a while ago by one of his workmates. Seems he was working on a building site, and managed to fall off some scaffolding. The only thing he's complaining of is a headache and a sore ankle.'

'Well, let's take a look.' Kate put the plates up on a screen and studied the X-rays in silence, leaning forward to trace the pattern of an irregular line. 'They did the sensible thing in bringing him in. There's a small fracture there, look. He may not be feeling it too much right now, but if he'd tried to walking on it for an hour or so, he certainly would have known about it.'

'We'll get it plastered up, then, Doctor.'

'I'll take a look at him and check that headache. Has he complained of nausea, dizziness?'

'He's not saying much at all.' Sister bustled

beside Kate, sweeping aside the curtains to enter the cubicle where the patient was lying on the couch, looking less than happy and feeling 'a bit queasy', he said.

Kate emerged from the cubicle five minutes later. 'Get him up to the ward as soon as you can, Sister. We'll keep him for twenty-four hours or so. The concussion is going to make him feel pretty groggy for a while.'

The arrival of an ambulance heralded another admission. The patient, an elderly lady, had slipped on a patch of ice, and was very distressed and in a great deal of pain. She was transferred carefully to a couch.

'Can't give you many details.' The porter handed a shopping bag to Sister. 'Keep an eye on that for her, will you? Seems she was doing a bit of shopping when she fell. Name's Mrs Prentice.'

'I'll see to it.' Sister Fields was rallying staff. 'Anyone with her? Relatives?'

'No, and the ambulance chaps couldn't get any information.'

'Well, leave it with us. She'll be pretty shocked.'

Kate, making a preliminary examination, was in silent agreement. Any fall was potentially dangerous in the elderly. Not just because of the injury, but because there was often a real danger of pneumonia setting in after the shock.

'Mrs Prentice?' She squeezed the woman's

frail hand gently. 'Do you know where you are?'

Watery blue eyes stared vaguely around the cubicle. 'Must have tripped. Hurt my leg.'

Kate's glance met Tony's as she moved out from behind the curtains. 'I'll have to get her admitted straight away and sort out the details later. She's in a pretty bad way. Her hip is fractured. We'll see precisely how bad the damage is when we get the X-rays. They're being done now.'

The phone was ringing in the office. A staff nurse sped away to deal with it, just as Tony was called away to deal with an unconscious child being carried into another cubicle.

For the next hour the whole department was stretched to capacity, until the rush suddenly seemed to peter out, leaving time to snatch a break. The coffee had just been poured when the emergency bleeper went off.

Tony groaned. 'Here we go again. Never a dull moment.'

Kate beat him to the door, meeting Sister as she came hurrying out of the office. 'RTA, Doctor. On the way in now.'

'How many?'

'Three stretcher cases that we know of. One severe spine and leg injuries. One head injury. No more details at the moment.'

'Right. Better alert the emergency team, and make sure we get blood off for cross-matching as soon as possible. Alert X-ray, will you, and get the mobile unit in. Any plates will need to be read and reported on immediately.'

Within minutes the first cases began to arrive. 'This is the head injury.' The ambulance team had done what they could to keep the unconscious man comfortable. An airway had been inserted, keeping him breathing, but only just.

Kate was checking the vital signs as he was transferred from the stretcher on to a waiting trolley. 'Get some sterile dressings on this wound and bleep Mr Francis—he'll want to see this one—and take a look at the X-rays before we move him up to Theatre.'

It seemed only seconds before the tall, grey-suited neuro-surgeon came striding into the department with Jim Lawson, the senior registrar, at his side.

'One for me, Doctor?'

Kate looked up and managed to smile. 'Could be more than one, I'm afraid. There's been a multiple pile-up. We're still not sure how many are coming in.'

Jim Lawson began his own swift examination. 'There's a nasty open fracture of the left leg that's going to need surgery. Could be a long job. There's bone all over the place.'

'Looks as if we'd better work on him together. If Theatre Two's empty we'll have him up there.'

'I checked, sir,' Sister said. 'It should be free in

about half an hour.'

They worked with speed and efficiency, Kate moving on to attend a young woman who lay on the couch, her eyes closed as staff nurse swabbed a wound which was bleeding profusely. Even the gentlest of movements drew a groan from the girl.

'This arm is broken.' Kate moved to a gash across her temple. 'This will need suturing. Hopefully it won't leave a scar.' She smiled down at the girl. 'All in all, you've been pretty lucky. We'll get you cleaned up and that arm in plaster. You should be able to home later.'

'Doctor—' Sister put her head round the curtains. 'One of the drivers has just been brought in. He's in a bad way.'

The stretcher was wheeled in, a staff nurse keeping the oxygen mask in place over the patient's nose and mouth as the porters deftly, manoeuvred the trolley into place. The man's face was tinged an unhealthy grey. Kate took one look at his erratic breathing and rapped out, 'He's arresting!'

Within seconds the room was full of people as the team worked in a controlled but desperate fight for the man's life. He must be about fifty, she guessed, though it was difficult to tell as the features took on the bluish colour of someone whose heart has ceased to beat.

Kate was aware of yet another figure moving beside her. Without looking up, she muttered her thanks as a pair of hands took over and she was able to east her cramped limbs. It was several tense minutes before the laboured breathing began again and the air of tension seemed visible to relax.

By now there were so many figures in the small area, as various members of the departments responded to the emergency call, that Kate scarcely noticed who they were.

'How's his blood pressure, Sister?' she asked.

'Rising, Doctor.'

'Keep checking.' She bent closer, applying a stethoscope to the man's chest, then reached for an ophthalmoscope, pausing to wipe the tiny beads of sweat from her brown. Suddenly the air in the small treatment are seemed stifling.

'Here, let me.'

She jerked back to reality only to feel herself tremble with shock as she found herself staring into a pair of sombre blue eyes. It wasn't possible . . . but she knew there was no doubt.

'I'm all right.'

Jake Ramsey took the ophthalmoscope from her numb fingers. She wanted to say something, anything. His gaze met hers above his mask, then his head was bent, before she had had time to guess what was going on behind, the, oh, so familiar blue eyes.

The shock of his nearness seemed to rob her of every shred of control. Several times their hands made contact, sending a tremor of shock running through her.

'He's lost a hell of a lot of blood. Get that sample off for cross-matching as fast as you can, Sister.' Jake stepped back, pulling the mask down from his face and revealing lines of weariness.

Kate's hands were still shaking as she unfastened her own mask. 'Jake.' There was a look of blatant appeal in her eyes as she stared up at him. 'We have to talk.'

He looked older. There were tiny lines of exhaustion round his eyes and mouth.

'Jake, there's a theatre free. I need you to scrub up.' Jim Lawson's voice came between them. She saw Jake's face darken, then, without a word, he turned and walked away.

She was sitting in the office, several hours later, trying to concentrate on writing up her reports, when the sound of her name being spoken brought her out of her reverie. She looked up to see Sister standing in the doorway.

'I'm sorry to disturb you, Doctor, but you're wanted urgently, up on men's surgical.'

It took a few seconds to shake off the feeling of lethargy, and for the words to penetrate her brain. 'Men's surgical? Are you sure?'

'Oh yes, Doctor. I took the message only a moment ago. Mr Collins is waiting for you.'

Kate was already heading for the door. Doctors didn't run except in cases of dire emergency, such

as multiple accidents or cardiac arrest, but
suddenly she was running, completely unaware of
the curious glances cast in her direction. Please
don't let it be, the silent thought kept running
through her head.

Steve Collins wasn't on the ward. He met her as
she came through the swing doors, took her arm
and guided her into the office which Sister had
vacated. One look at her pale face and darkly
shadowed eyes was enough to tell him that she
was putting her own professional interpretation on
the reason for his call. He closed the door quietly.

'There's no easy way to put this. Your father had
a coronary, about fifteen minutes ago.'

Her hands clenched. 'Is he . . .?'

'He's fighting.' The young cardiologist was
quietly reassuring. 'It happened very quickly,
but the resuscitation team were there within
seconds. For a while it was touch and go, but
he rallied.'

Kate was on her feet. 'I'd like to see him.'

'Yes, of course, but just for a few seconds. You
don't need me to tell you the risks. He's very ill,
but we're keeping him monitored and you have
my word that if there's even the slightest change,
you'll be called.'

'I'd really rather stay, if not with him, then at
least close by.'

'I wouldn't advise it and it certainly wouldn't
serve any purpose.' His tone softened. 'You know

the procedures. We'll be keeping him sedated. The best thing you can do, for his sake and your own, is to go home and try to get some rest. Come in later, by all means, but he's going to be in a fairly critical state for several days.'

She was vaguely aware of the door opening behind her and of someone else coming into the room as he exchanged a look with whomever it was. Thinking it was Sister, she didn't look up.

'I can't force you to go.' Steve Collins was saying. 'But you can help most by letting us do our job, and now I'd better get back and take another look at him.'

It was the gentlest of professional dismissals. Kate turned unsteadily. The figure at the door moved. Jake's face swam into view. His face was gaunt, but her stricken gaze hardly registered such things as she stared at him, then, with a sob, went into the refuge of his arms.

'Jake. Oh, Jake!'

He was speaking softly as he held her, feeling his own throat tighten in painful spasms. 'It's going to be all right, Kate,' his voice rasped.

Steve Collins slipped quietly away, leaving them alone.

'I can't believe you're here.' Her voice was muffled as he held her close. 'I thought . . . I thought you didn't want to see me.'

His mouth came down on hers with a sense of

urgency so great that she moaned softly, hardly recognising the sound as coming from herself.

His face was grim as he released her mouth but held her tight in his arms. 'Don't say another word. If you knew how I had to fight the temptation to take you in my arms, down there, in front of everyone, and make love to you, not even knowing whether you'd welcome me or hate me . . .'

They clung together, her body offering no resistance against the urgency she sensed in him now. 'How could I hate you?' she murmured throatily.

'I love you, Kate,' he said hoarsely, then his hands tightened on her arms. 'Come on, I'm taking you home. We've got a lot of talking to do, and this isn't the place for the things I have to say, to explain.'

'But Dad . . .'

'You can pop in and say goodnight as we leave,'

Twenty minutes later they were in the car, driving through the late night traffic.

Kate shivered.

'Cold?'

'No, not really.' She was so glad to have him there, just sitting beside her. Never in her life had she been so glad of the shadows that hid her from him, yet allowed her to take in every detail of his profile, the taut, lean frame. It was as if she could actually draw strength simply from his nearness. And that was the miracle she still couldn't understand. When she needed him most he was there. She was almost afraid to close her eyes, in case, when she opened them again, he would be gone and it would all turn out to have been a dream. She preferred to fight the feeling of exhaustion that was threatening to wash over her.

When Kate opened her eyes ten minutes later, however, Jake was still very much there. It was only as she sat up, rubbing her eyes to look round her, that realised they were not where she expected to be.

'I thought you were taking me home.'

'I am,' he reassured her. 'This is my home.'

She felt his gaze on her, sensed his tension and guessed the reason for it. Without a word she took his hand and let him lead her, through the light flurry of snow which had begun to fall, into the warmth.

Stepping inside, he closed the door, and drew into his arms. It was like coming home in more senses that one, Kate thought dreamily as they finally, gently, broke the contact between them, her lips still throbbing from the intensity of his kiss. With a sigh of pleasure she buried her face against his neck. 'Oh, Jake . . .' She clung to him.

'I didn't think this would ever happen,' he said in a small, tight voice. 'I thought I'd thrown it all away. The day I watched you leave the island . . . If there really is a hell, I knew then what it must be like.'

Kate stared at him, confused. 'Jake, I don't understand. I'm afraid you're going to have to explain.'

'That's the reason I brought you here, one of the reasons.' He eased himself free of her, leading her into a sitting-room. A fire, blazing in the hearth, gave the only light but he made no attempt to light the lamps, and Kate was glad. She wanted to ask what the other reason was, but her voice seemed to be trapped somewhere in her throat.

'Let me take you coat. Sit down. I'll pour you a drink.'

She didn't want a drink, she wanted to be in his arms. He left for a few seconds, returning with a glass in his hand.

'Here, drink this. It's brandy. It will do you good.'

'But aren't you having one?'

He shook his head. 'If there's any chance you may need to go back to the hospital, I'm driving you.'

Her throat tightened. She took a sip of the drink, then put the glass down. Her eyes locked with his across the room. 'I don't need a drink, Jake. I need you,' she said, brokenly.

He gazed into her eyes, then, almost hesitantly, he moved towards her and Kate ran to him to be enfolded in his arms.

'Kate, oh, Kate. If you knew how much I wanted you. Every time I came near you, it was as much as I could do to keep my hands off you, to stop myself taking you to bed and making love to you.'

'Then why didn't you?' she asked breathlessly, as soon as he released her mouth from his.

For a moment his gaze was uncertain as he looked down at her. 'Because I was a fool. Because I didn't know for sure that was what you wanted and because . . . I was afraid to find out.'

Kate swallowed nervously, her hands reaching up to smooth the hair back from his forehead. 'Jake, Sam told me . . . about your wife, about Helen.' She had to catch her lower lip between her teeth to stop it trembling. 'You must have loved her very much,' she managed at last.

'I did,' he said hoarsely. 'She was a lovely person. It was very easy to love her. When she died . . .'

'Jake, you don't have to talk about it.'

'I think it's time I did,' he murmured. 'When Helen died I swore no one would ever take her place. I didn't believe anyone ever could. Yet suddenly you were there and, for the first time since her death, I began to feel that my loyalty to her was being threatened.'

'There's nothing wrong with that,' Kate whispered.

His hands tightened on her arms. 'There's everything wrong with it. I didn't believe I had the right to let myself fall in love again. I fought against it, told myself I wanted you, even needed you, but it couldn't be love.'

Kate felt her heart racing. Her body ached with needs of her own. 'When did you decide you were wrong?'

'The minute I realised I'd let you go, probably for ever. I knew then that I must have fallen in love with you the minute I saw you, that day when you came walking out of the sea, with a flower tucked behind your ear.' His hands cupped her face, his eyes darkening as he looked at her. 'I'm almost afraid to touch you,' he murmured huskily. 'I'm afraid to ask whether it's too late?'

Kate felt the tears of happiness fill her eyes. 'I love you,' she whispered. 'Even when I thought you were still married to Helen.'

Anguish briefly distorted his features. 'You thought that? Oh, my dear love——'

She silenced him by placing a hand over his mouth. 'It seems we were both fighting for the wrong reasons, but I don't think Helen would have wanted us to be unhappy, do you?'

'I can't pretend I don't love you,' he said huskily. 'I have to have you in my life.' His voice was ragged with worry. 'I want you to marry me. I can't take any chance of losing you again.'

Kate drew his head down until their lips met in a gentle kiss. 'Or course I'll marry you.' She heard him groan softly, then his kiss became more demanding until finally, reluctantly, he broke away.

'There's one other thing I should tell you. I've

been offered a new job, and it's too good to turn
down.'

Kate stiffened in his arms. Dazed, she frowned
up at him. 'A job? Where? What kind of job?'

He tilted her chin, teasing a strand of hair from
her cheek. 'I'm afraid it will mean some travelling,
I've been asked to take over a new hospital.'

Kate swallowed hard. 'When?'

'It should be ready in about six months, but I'll
need to do a visit before then, just to make sure
everything is progressing as it should. Of course,
I'll need to take my new assistant with me.'

Her head jerked up. 'And is this going to be
before or after we're married?'

His voice grew husky. 'I was hoping it would be
after, my darling. That way I thought we could
make the trip part of our honeymoon.'

Her eyes flew wide. 'Honeymoon? But . . . Jake
Ramsey, what are you trying to say? I have no
intention of sharing my honeymoon with your
new assistant! Wh . . . where is this hospital
anyway?'

He drew her roughly towards him, imprisoning
her in the circle of his arms. 'I thought you'd guess,'
he muttered. 'I've been asked to go back to the
island, to take over the new hospital that's being
built there. In six months' time, your father should
be well on the road to recovery.'

Kate felt suddenly very much in need of her
brandy. 'Oh, Jake.' She gazed at him, her eyes

shining.

'Oh, Kate,' he muttered savagely. 'I think we'd better get married right away.'

'But what about this new assistant?'

A nerve pulsed his jaw. 'Well, I suppose if you don't want the job, I can always find someone else, but I rather thought you'd like the idea. Just for a couple of years, until our first little islander comes along.'

'Don't you dare, Jake Ramsey. Don't you . . .' She sighed dreamily as his mouth came down on hers. 'I wonder if there are blue flowers on the island, as well as pink?' she murmured thoughtfully, when he finally let her go.

ROMANCING THE PHONE

Win the romantic holiday of a lifetime for two at the exclusive Couples Hotel in Ocho Rios on Jamaica's north coast with the Mills & Boon and British Telecom's novel competition, 'Romancing the Phone'.

This exciting competition looks at the importance the telephone call plays in romance. All you have to do is write a story or extract about a romance involving the phone which lasts approximately two minutes when read aloud.

The winner will not only receive the holiday in Jamaica, but the entry will also be heard by millions of people when it is included in a selection of extracts from a short list of entries on British Telecom's 'Romance Line'. Regional winners and runners up will receive British Telecom telephones, answer machines and Mills & Boon books.

For an entry leaflet and further details all you have to do is call 01 400 5359, or write to 'Romancing the Phone', 22 Endell Street, London WC2H 9AD.

You may be mailed with other offers as a result of this application.

Unwrap romance this Christmas

A Love Affair
LINDSAY ARMSTRONG

Valentine's Night
PENNY JORDAN

Man on the Make
ROBERTA LEIGH

Rendezvous in Rio
ELIZABETH OLDFIELD

Put some more romance into your Christmas, with four brand new titles from Mills & Boon in this stylish gift pack.

They make great holiday reading, and for only £5.40 it makes an ideal gift.

The special gift pack is available from 6th October Look out for it at Boots, Martins, John Menzies, W.H. Smith, Woolworths and other paperback stockists.